SOUTHERN MAGIC THANKSGIVING

SWEET TEA WITCH MYSTERIES BOOK SEVEN

AMY BOYLES

ONE

"*H*urry up! We've got to get the frozen turkeys hidden."

I stared at the brick-hard bird carcasses in my shopping cart. It was ridiculous enough that I was pushing a grocery buggy in the park behind Bubbling Cauldron Road. Much less the fact that it was filled with twenty-pound turkeys.

"Why are we hiding turkeys, again?" I said.

My grandmother, Betty Craple, glared at me through silver-framed glasses. She wore rainbow-striped knee socks that hit the hem of her beige skirt. If the stripes weren't bad enough, wooden clogs had swallowed her feet. My grandmother loved nothing if not seventies clothing. Do not ask me why.

"Kid, I thought I explained this to you," she said.

I hitched a shoulder and gave her an apologetic smile. "I don't think so. I must've missed something."

"All right. But hurry up with that cart." I gave the buggy one good shove and caught up with her. "Every year Magnolia Cove hosts a Thanksgiving turkey hunt on Thanksgiving Eve."

I stopped pushing to chew my lower lip. There were limitless responses to her statement. Ever since I'd moved to Magnolia Cove, I'd realized this town was a teensy bit different from most.

No, it wasn't simply the fact that it was a town full of witches and that only witches could enter. When it came to holidays, Magnolia Cove did things right.

At Halloween the town contracted cat-sized spiders and actual ghosts for their haunted house. If they did that for Halloween, what did the town do on Thanksgiving?

Apparently, hold a frozen turkey hunt.

I paused. "Okay, wait. Now this makes no sense. The town holds a turkey hunt? Aren't y'all getting your holidays confused? It should be an Easter egg hunt on Easter. Not a turkey hunt on gobble-gobble day."

She sighed with annoyance, as if I were supposed to know the inner workings of a town I'd only lived in a few months. "Used to be some folks were poor. We started the turkey hunt as a way to give everyone a chance of having a bird to eat on Thanksgiving."

"It's a town full of witches who work magic," I argued. "They can create a turkey out of air. Or better yet, why don't you just go door-to-door and hand out birds?"

Betty pointed to a spot behind a bench. "Put one there."

I heaved a twenty-pound Butterball from the cart and dropped it with a thud onto the yellowing grass. "Anyone can steal it."

Betty waved a hand over the carcass. Magical dust appeared from nowhere and coated it. "This will keep it frozen and safe until tomorrow."

"I still don't understand this," I grumbled.

She shot me a scathing look. "Listen, kid, you gotta get out of this funk."

"I'm not in a funk."

She rolled her eyes. Why was it when old ladies rolled their eyes, it was always much more dramatic, like they had the wisdom of the world in their brain or something?

"Ever since that boyfriend of yours left town, you've been depressed."

I shoved the cart for emphasis. "I haven't been depressed. The last thing I've been is depressed. See that squirrel in that tree?" I said, pointing to a rodent biting through a nut. "I'm as carefree as that critter."

"What? You gonna sit around and chomp nuts all day?"

"No," I said, annoyed. "I'm not going to eat nuts all day."

"That's good. They've got too much fat in them. Might add a few pounds to those hips of yours." She nodded toward a hill. "Come on. We've got more turkeys to plant."

I pushed the cart with more force than I needed to. She threw me a pointed glance.

I wasn't upset. I was fine. I hadn't cried in weeks. I considered that a win.

Yes, I was emotionally twisted. Yes, I was so full of anger and sadness that I wanted to throw rocks off a mountain. But overall I'd been doing great, shoving my frustration down to the pit of my stomach.

Hadn't I?

I pedaled my feet to catch up. "Listen, I'm fine. Just because Axel said he couldn't be around me and had to leave forever, that doesn't mean I'm shattered."

Betty's gaze slid to study me. "Whatever you say, kid."

"I've been fine, Betty."

"Sure."

I stopped and raised my hands. "Okay. That's it. Fess up. Tell me everything. Stop pussyfooting around what it is you want to say. I'm a big girl; I can take it."

Betty cracked her knuckles and rolled her shoulders as if she were preparing to sprint into the Magnolia Cove Marathon. Okay, I didn't know if that was a thing, but I wouldn't put it past Betty to start one next week if I mentioned it.

She pressed a finger to her nose. Three turkeys rose from the cart and sailed to spots in the park. One landed behind a mailbox, another behind a light pole and the third rested behind a fountain featuring a unicorn.

"Kid, ever since Axel left, you've been moping around. You don't open your mouth unless you're forced into it."

"Work's keeping me busy."

She shot me another dark look. "Busy feeding dogs and cats every day? All day?"

Okay, so I'd been spending some time at Familiar Place. But I owned the store. "I need to make sure they're taken care of."

"And when your cousins invite you out to do things, you always say no."

"I don't always say no."

Betty glared at me.

I threw up my hands. "So they asked me shopping and to a movie. I didn't feel like going, all right?"

She fisted her hands to her hips and planted her feet wide. Oh no, this was it. I was about to get full-on Betty Craple. She might be so ticked a tornado would shoot straight out of her head.

"Kid, you've got to get over it. Axel is a great man, but has he contacted you at all?"

My stomach fell to my feet. Not in three weeks, he hadn't. Axel Reign, my boyfriend—okay, at this point my ex—had dumped me on November first, the day after we fixed a huge Halloween blunder. We'd solved it and he'd dumped me.

Of course, he hadn't dumped me just because he felt like it. See, Axel is half wizard, half werewolf. He'd shifted into his wolf form and attacked and almost killed me.

I'd tried to tell him it was no big deal, that I could wear my big-girl panties and handle it, but he kinda took the whole I-almost-ripped-out-your-throat thing to heart. So much so that he dumped me and ditched Magnolia Cove.

For good.

My heart squeezed. It felt like giant hands were wringing all the blood from it. So what that only the day before Axel left, I'd confessed that I loved him? He'd told me the same. So what that I felt like my heart had been torn from my throat and squashed?

Wasn't a girl allowed a little time to mourn?

But apparently that time now edged on three weeks of moping. I dressed daily, thank you very much. I managed to brush my hair nearly every day. I might've missed a Sunday or two, but who was counting?

Apparently, Betty Craple.

"Has he contacted you?" she repeated.

I pursed my lips because I sure as all get-out didn't want to confess the absolute rock bottom, stupid truth of the matter. No, Axel Reign had not bothered to pick up a phone, dial my number and listen to the sound of my sweet voice.

There were a lot of words in my head about that, but none of them were nice, so I will not be doing any sharing.

"Morning, y'all!"

Betty and I turned to see a woman with long chestnut hair waving. She wore high-heeled brown boots, chocolate-colored leggings and a red over-the-shoulder T-shirt.

The breeze picked up her hair. It floated like magic behind her. She managed the divots and dips in the grass like a professional, sashaying quickly to us.

Gold bangles lined both her arms. She hoisted a pile of baker's boxes into an opposite arm before pushing her sunglasses up on her head.

"Morning," she repeated.

I shot Betty a look that said, *who's that?* Betty answered with a slight hitch of her shoulder.

Since it never killed anyone to smile, though it might hurt if I'd had a tooth worked on and the tetracaine was wearing off, I forced myself to put on my whitest and brightest.

"Morning," I said.

The woman extended a long, lithe arm. "Is this where the turkey hunt's going to be tomorrow?"

Betty fisted her hands to her hips. "Who wants to know?"

There goes early-morning diplomacy.

"Ah am so sorry," she said. The woman had a thick country Southern accent. I wouldn't have been surprised if she told me her name was Bubba. "I'm Lori Lou Fick."

"I'm Pepper Dunn," I said. I glanced at Betty, waiting for her to introduce herself. She clamped her lips. I wrapped an arm around her and squeezed my grandmother gently. "This is Betty Craple."

"I opened the new pie and sweet shop—The Sweet Witch. It's over on Bubbling Cauldron."

"New sweet shop?" I said.

"And pies." Lori Lou thrust out the boxes. I peered inside. Sure enough, a pecan pie sat squarely inside. But in the very center of the pie lay a chocolate bat.

"Carmen Craple is the only person who owns a sweet shop in Magnolia Cove," Betty said, practically snarling.

I nudged my grandmother and gave her a look that said, *be nice.* "I'm sure Magnolia Cove would love to have a bakery."

"Yes, we had a great first day yesterday. That's when folks told me about the turkey hunt, and I thought I'd put some pies out to be hunted as well. You know, it's good advertising for me."

She pointed one trendy-colored black fingernail at the box. A gold sticker took up the entire top. In scrolling purple script were the words THE SWEET WITCH.

Betty's face crimsoned. Her eyes bugged, and a vessel throbbed in her temple. She was about to blow. My grandmother was about to lose her shinola, and I knew exactly why.

Betty Craple ran this town. This was her turkey hunt. *Hers.* No brand-spanking-new arrivals were allowed to hijack her tradition.

Betty jutted out her chin. "This hunt is for turkeys only."

Lori Lou smiled slightly. Her brown eyes glittered. "Well, I understand that this is y'all's whole big Thanksgiving thang. I thought it'd be nice to add some pies. Trust me, you'll love them. Here. Have one on me."

She thrust a box into Betty's stomach. My grandmother had no choice but to take it.

Lori Lou gave a finger wave. "Now you enjoy that. While you do, I'll be going around and hiding the rest of these in preparation for tomorrow. It was so nice meetin' y'all. And be sure to come check out the shop. We've got lots of wonderful treats."

With that, Miss Lori Lou Fick, newcomer and interloper in

Magnolia Cove, Alabama, trotted off to ruin Betty's Thanksgiving Eve frozen turkey hunt.

Betty's face was a burning shade of red.

"You okay?" I placed a hand on her shoulder.

She shot the pie in her hands a look of disgust. "Who does that woman think she is?"

"Magnolia Cove's new master baker."

My grandmother's lower lip trembled. "We'll see about that. Soon as she's gone, I'm going to take every last pie she hides and throw them in the trash."

I tempered the laugh that threatened to bubble from my lips. "Now Betty, that's not a very good attitude."

She snorted. "Forget the season of giving. I'm the only person who runs this town."

Lori Lou's bottom wiggled this way and that as she dropped a pie on the ground. "Sorry, Betty, but it looks like you lost your title to a woman named Lori Lou."

Betty's brow wrinkled to a deep furrow. "We'll see about that."

TWO

"*G*irls, we've got a problem."

It was suppertime. To lots of folks that would be "dinner," but in the South dinner is actually lunch and supper is supper.

Betty stood in front of the hearth. The ever-burning fire was spitting nails, it was hissing and crackling so fierce.

My grandmother gnashed the corncob pipe between her teeth. She pulled out a pouch of tobacco and ignited it, blowing smoke the shape of turkeys to the ceiling.

My cousin Amelia sat on the couch shelling hazelnuts and popping them in her mouth one at a time. "What sort of problem?"

"There's a new witch in town trying to hijack the Thanksgiving Turkey Hunt."

"She must not know you." My other cousin Cordelia sat in a chair thumbing the screen on her phone.

Betty poked the air with her pipe. "She doesn't know me. That's the problem. Came into the park and started hiding pecan pies. *Pecan pies*," she stressed, as if it were the worst catastrophe to ever hit Magnolia Cove.

I knew for a fact that wasn't true. That had occurred on Halloween

8

when time had stopped. Anyway, that was another story for another time.

I glimpsed myself in a mirror. My honey and crimson hair was frizzed on the ends. My brown eyes peeked out from under freshly trimmed bangs, and I had deep purple cups under my eyes.

I hadn't been sleeping, not since this whole thing with Axel, but I wasn't going to admit that to anybody.

I slumped onto the couch. "I don't get what the big deal is. She's new in town and wants to help out. What's the harm in that?"

As if on cue, the front door blew open. My cousin Carmen Craple whisked inside, escorting a cool breeze with her.

"Y'all, I'm trying not to freak out, but I'm freaking out."

I shot Amelia and Cordelia concerned looks. In all the months I'd known Carmen, she was cool as cucumber water. Seriously. The woman never ruffled.

"What's wrong?" Amelia said.

Carmen raked her fingers through her red locks. I made room for her on the couch, and she sank onto a cushion, placing her hands on her knees. Her breathing came fast and furious. She hiccuped several times before exhaling deeply.

"I don't know what's come over me. Look, I'm shaking." She leveled a hand, and sure enough, she was trembling like a mouse cornered by a cat.

"It's just, the new shop that's opened up in town—The Sweet Witch. It's stealing all my business."

"No way," Amelia said. "You make the best sweets in town."

"I thought I did," Carmen said, "but this week is supposed to be one of my busiest—I've got pumpkin any which way you can imagine —and I'm sinking. I can't even sell a dozen pumpkin-spiced cookies."

I grimaced. My gaze snagged on Betty, who was giving me a *what-did-I-tell-you* look.

Amelia thumbed toward me. "Betty and Pepper met her today."

Carmen's gaze zeroed on me. "You met her?" I swear, her voice rose several octaves.

Heat flushed my neck. Had the room warmed up? I felt all eyes on me, as if I were some sort of spy who had primo intelligence on the whole situation.

I cleared my throat, hoping everyone would stop staring. Wishful thinking as their gazes bored harder. "Her name's Lori Lou. Betty and I met her at the park by Bubbling Cauldron."

"She's sabotaging the turkey hunt," Betty snapped. "Hiding pies. Well, I'll tell Miss Lori Lou where she can hide a pie."

Cordelia gave Betty the hand stop signal. "Hold on there. She's only trying to help."

"Help?" Betty shouted. "She opens a shop across from Carmen's the week of Thanksgiving, steals all her customers and then crashes my hunt. Mine. I plan it. I do it. Every year."

I wanted to rake my fingers down my face. It was only a turkey hunt. Nothing to get your panties in a wad about. Course, I wasn't going to tell Betty that. She might eat my face.

Yes, she was that ticked.

"Carmen, it can't be that bad," Amelia said. "You always do great business Thanksgiving week."

She smacked her lips. "I usually do. But if business keeps up the way it is, this new shop is going to run me straight out of town."

Amelia pointed to the dining table. "Lori Lou-hoo or whoever gave Pepper a pie."

Carmen shot me a look full of flamethrowers. "What?"

I coughed into my hand. "She gave it to Betty, actually. We didn't buy it. There. Take a look."

The four of us circled around the baker's box. From her perch on a chair, Mattie the Talking Cat opened one eye and then the other. "What's all the fuss, y'all?"

"That pie," I said.

"Oh, that pretty one with the chocolate bat cooked into the center?"

Carmen's eye twitched. "A chocolate bat in the center? I do that. I do that to my pecan pies, too."

Uh-oh. This was going very bad.

"I'm sure it's horrible," Cordelia said. "It's probably not any good."

Amelia rubbed Carmen's shoulder. "None of us are going to eat it. We're not traitors. In fact"—she lifted it from the table and marched to the kitchen—"I'm throwing it away."

An idea flashed bright and white in my head. I hooked an arm around Carmen. "Tell you what, cuz, tomorrow I'll take a look and see who's actually going into the new shop and find out if you're really in trouble or not."

Carmen nibbled her bottom lip. "Think it'll help?"

"Sure," Betty said. "We'll blackmail folks and keep 'em at your place."

Finally Carmen cracked a smile. "You don't have to."

I hugged my cousin. "I'm happy to help. You'll see. It won't be nearly as big a problem as you think."

BUT IT WAS A BIG PROBLEM. Huge, in fact. It was the morning of Thanksgiving Eve. I know that's not a thing like Christmas Eve, but you know it's still kind of a holiday.

Folks were flooding into Magnolia Cove to visit family. The holidays are a big deal. More folks present meant more traffic and more witches looking for familiars.

The whole shebang means I must work my tail ragged to keep up with the commotion in my shop.

Anyway, that's where we were—Cordelia, Amelia, Mattie and I. We were inside Familiar Place stalking the Sweet Witch because I had a great view of the store from my front windows.

"Oh my gosh, is that Sylvia Spirits?" Amelia said.

Sure enough, Sylvia Spirits, owner of Charming Conical Caps, was heading into the new bakery.

"She loves Carmen's treats," Cordelia said.

Mattie licked her paw. "Ain't nothin' like a shiny new diamond to steal a woman's attention."

I frowned. "Are you calling the shop a diamond?"

"It's a trinket, ain't it? New and fabulous. Folks are going to check it out."

"And bankrupting Carmen in the meantime," Cordelia said.

Amelia gave our cousin a look filled with shock. "Are you actually worried about Carmen?"

"Of course I'm worried. I don't want our cousin to suffer. Why?" she said in a grouchy voice.

"It's just so strange of you to be concerned and not bored out of your mind."

Cordelia jabbed Amelia in the arm.

"Ouch," Amelia said.

"I can be nice," Cordelia said.

"Pretty sure that's case in point that you've got a mean streak," I said.

Cordelia glared at me but said nothing. Instead she threw up her hands. "Okay, what do y'all want? For me to blow sunshine and rainbows out of my butt?"

"Yes," Amelia said. "That would be pretty cool."

"It might kill me," Cordelia said.

I laughed. I grabbed my Styrofoam cup of sweet tea and sipped. It was sweet but missing something. I riffled through my purse.

"Crap, I'm out of jelly beans."

"I'm sure Carmen has some," Cordelia said.

"Yeah, and she could probably use the business."

I eyed the steady stream of folks spilling from the Sweet Witch. Anyone and everyone was taking a turn going in and out. It was so busy I was surprised that folks weren't tailgating out of their pickup trucks while they waited to buy a pie.

Just kidding. But it was busy.

I was about to enter Carmen's store, Marshmallow Magic, when a tall man wearing a white apron flew out of the Sweet Witch. He didn't actually fly, but that was certainly something you could expect in Magnolia Cove. You know, with the whole town being full of witches and all.

He was tall with a mop of brown hair. He took one step forward and paused, seeming to think better of his decision. He whirled around, yanked open the door and yelled, "Move your garbage from my back door! I won't tell y'all again!"

He slammed the door and turned away, heading around the corner.

My heart raced from watching the interaction. "Who was that?"

Amelia's eyes widened to saucers. "That's Parker Moody. Owns Magical Moonshine."

"Magical Moonshine?" I said.

She nodded. "It's fairly new. I haven't been in, but apparently he gives free tastings."

"What's the moonshine supposed to do?" Cordelia said. "Give you magical beer goggles?"

I laughed. It was an old joke that beer goggles made anyone look good. Which meant if you were tipsy enough and it was New Year's Eve, even a homeless man would look good enough to smooch for good luck.

Yuck.

"Not everyone's been taken with the Sweet Witch. Wonder what she did to tick Parker off," I murmured.

We entered Carmen's shop. The shop was quiet as a funeral wake with a side buffet filled with food.

I mean, y'all, you could have heard half a pin drop.

"Morning." Carmen's voice finally filled the void of silence.

"Morning," I said.

My cousins exchanged greetings as I wandered the store. The place was jam-packed with goodies for the holidays—pumpkin pies, pumpkin cookies, pumpkin meringues. Everything was either pie or pumpkin shaped. There were pumpkin cream cheese Swiss rolls, turkey cookies—literally a mountain of delicious sugar that was ready to be bought and devoured by half of town.

But no one was buying.

"I came for some jelly beans," I said.

Carmen flashed me a gorgeous smile. "I've got brand-new fall flavors, just for you, Pepper."

Delight sparked in me. Childlike glee filled me from head to foot. Yes, over jelly beans. I loved them so.

Carmen pointed to a wire rack. "I made pumpkin spiced, cranberry, cornbread dressing if you want something more savory. There's apple pie, cinnamon latte and even honey cake."

I picked a cellophane bag filled with darkly colored red, green and yellow beans. "Wow, you've outdone yourself. Those sound delicious. How much for two bags?"

Carmen waved me away. "On the house."

I frowned. "No. I want to pay for it."

For goodness' sake, Carmen's store was empty. I didn't want her business to go belly up because I didn't buy a bag of jelly beans. Yes, I know that was silly and stupid, but I wanted to contribute.

Carmen's eyes sparkled with mischief. "I know what you're thinking. That you want to pay. I want you to, but not with money."

Cordelia and Amelia drifted over to us. I shot them a glance, but both my cousins hitched their shoulders. They didn't know what Carmen was talking about any more than I did.

Mattie the Cat jumped up on the windowsill. She gave me a bored stare before proceeding to clean her face.

"What do you mean, Carmen?" I said.

She hesitated.

Mattie spoke up. "What your cousin is afraid to say is that she wants y'all to go on over to that shop and snoop around, find out what the big deal is."

Amelia's eyes flashed to Carmen. "You want us to spy?"

"Yep," Carmen said. "It would be awesome if you did."

I dropped the jelly beans in my purse and flashed Carmen a huge smile. "Why, cuz, we'd be happy to."

THREE

By the time we reached the Sweet Witch—and I'm talking it was only a few seconds later—the line wound out the door. We stood amid a throng of locals.

"I feel like a traitor," Amelia said.

"We're spying," Cordelia whispered.

Amelia clapped lightly with glee. "You mean we're like secret agents? Like that Jack Ryan guy on that television show?"

"Just like it," Cordelia said with a heavy dollop of sarcasm.

While they chatted, I watched the folks leaving. They were all smiling. Like really grinning wide and holding doors for each other and letting one another go first and stuff.

"Everyone's in a good mood," I murmured.

"Spirit of giving," Amelia said over my shoulder. "Tomorrow is Thanksgiving."

"And today is the turkey hunt," Cordelia said. "They're probably in a good mood because of that."

"Maybe," I said.

When we finally got inside, Cindy Lou Hoo—or Lori Lou, I should say—greeted us with a wide smile.

"Welcome, y'all. Pepper, it's so good to see you." She wiggled her fashionably black-lacquered nails at me. "What can I get for y'all today?"

I scanned the cases of pies and tarts, cookies, cupcakes and muffins. "What's the best thing on the menu?"

"Well, that would be the pumpkin pie, of course."

The voice came from beside the case. I glanced at it, but no one was standing there. At least, no one who was my height or taller. My gaze drifted down until it rested on a bunny rabbit.

A bunny rabbit. In a bakery.

The rabbit, dressed in a green waistcoat, hopped around to the front of the case. "Like I said, the best thing is the pumpkin pie."

"Oh my God, is that a talking rabbit?" Amelia said.

"No, it's a talking monkey," Cordelia replied.

Amelia shot our cousin a look that should've burned her to a crisp. "I was only wondering."

Lori Lou gestured to the rabbit. "Y'all, this is Collinsworth. He's my work rabbit."

"Work rabbit?" I said.

"Yes," Collinsworth said in a distinctly British accent. "I help Lori Lou and Becky Ray with whatever they need." He bowed. "I'm generally their official sniffer, but I often do other things for them, like guide them down the street and make sure they don't trip on stones."

"But you're not blind," Amelia said to Lori Lou. "You don't look blind."

Lori Lou smiled vacantly and pointed to the animal license on the board. "He's my helper rabbit. I have needs other than sight that Collinsworth assists with."

"And who's Becky Ray?"

Right on cue a thick woman with her hair tucked beneath a chef's hat appeared from the back carrying a tray of cheesecakes. She dropped them on the counter and dusted her hands.

Lori Lou wrapped an arm around the woman's shoulders. "This is Becky Ray, my sister."

"Hey," Becky Ray said in a deep, uninterested voice.

Lori Lou patted her shoulders. "Becky's not much for talk. She's more the workhorse of the business."

"Could y'all please hurry it up? I've got somewhere to be."

Cordelia, Amelia and I turned our heads at a snail's pace to the left. Standing behind us, tapping his foot impatiently, stood a fashionably dressed thirtyish man in a tweed jacket.

"Dicky Downy," Cordelia said. "I didn't know you liked sweets so much that you had to return to Magnolia Cove once a year to bless us with your presence."

Dicky Downy stared blankly at my cousin. "I just moved back." Dicky's gaze swept to me. He was good-looking but clearly full of himself.

Collinsworth the Rabbit hopped on the counter. I almost vomited. I had rabbits at the store. Sold them, in fact, as familiars, and they could poop, y'all. Breed and poop. That's what rabbits did best. Just watching Collinsworth in his waistcoat hopping around on counters in his bare feet was enough to make the acid in my stomach curdle to cottage cheese.

"I have Mr. Downy's order right here," Collinsworth said. "I believe it was a pecan pie."

Dicky stepped forward, arms outstretched. "That's right." He took the box and moved away. Then he stopped and stepped forward. "Hey, I didn't order a chocolate bat on it."

Lori Lou, her face bright with angst, leaned over the counter. "That's how we make it. You ordered the specialty, I think."

He frowned. "Yeah. It better taste okay or else I'll be back."

"It'll taste wonderful," Collinsworth said. "Perfect."

Dicky Downy gave me and my cousins the once-over. His gaze snagged on Amelia, and something tweaked in his eyes. "Good to see y'all again. Be running into you around town."

Amelia audibly swallowed. "Sure thing, Dicky."

Dicky vanished out the door, and I stepped forward. "Just give us a pumpkin pie. That'll be perfect."

Collinsworth wrapped up a pie with his furry little paws. We paid and left, going the long way around so no one noticed us running straight back to Carmen's store to taste test the sample.

It sort of worked. We entered Familiar Place, sneaked out the back and into Carmen's. I almost felt bad about keeping my shop closed half the morning, but it would be fine. I'd open for the afternoon. Hopefully some folks would enter and I'd be able to match a witch with his or her familiar.

Carmen was ready with forks. She handed me a sweet tea that she'd made, and I dropped several of my new flavors of jelly beans in. I waited for a few to dissolve and sipped.

Hmmm. Apple and cinnamon tea—heaven in Styrofoam.

"So how was it in there?" Carmen asked.

Amelia gestured wildly. "Let me tell you, it was crazy."

Carmen quirked an interested brow. "How?"

Amelia nudged my elbow. "Tell her, Pepper."

"What? Why me? Why should I tell her?"

"Because," Cordelia said smoothly, "you'll actually make sense. Amelia will flail around and screw up the story. She'll get all flustered."

Amelia nodded. "For once I agree with Cordelia."

"Um, okay, well…it was busy."

Mattie jumped on a chair. "They got a cotton-pickin' helper rabbit in there who wears clothes and speaks with a fake British accent."

Cordelia burst into laughter. She knuckled a tear from her eyes. "I'm so glad someone had the eggs to say it."

Carmen dropped a fork. It clattered on the counter. "You're kidding me. A rabbit?"

"Yes," I said, "I think it's part of the appeal of the place. A British-accented rabbit dishing up pie and country speak like he knows anything about Magnolia Cove."

"Oh, and that's not all," Amelia said. "Dicky Downy's back in town."

Carmen's brows shot to peaks. "Dicky Downy? You're kidding."

I made a stop gesture. "Okay, y'all. What's the big deal about Dicky Downy?"

Carmen coiled her arms over her breasts and sank onto one hip. "When we were growing up, Dicky Downy was the richest kid in town. Threw the biggest parties when his parents were gone, which was like every other weekend. He had a habit of also selling things on the side."

"Pot?" I said. I mean, all the cool kids in high school—at least all the rich ones—always seemed to have a side hustle of drug dealing. Don't ask me how it worked out that way, but it generally did.

"He didn't sell drugs," Carmen said. "He sold magic spells."

"What kind of spells?" I said.

"Love potions," Amelia said.

Cordelia leaned a hip against the counter. "And from the look of things, whatever love spell he cast on Amelia all those years ago is still going strong."

"I don't know what you're talking about," Amelia said, sniffing.

Cordelia scoffed. "Right. He looked you up and down like you were a frozen popsicle in the middle of the desert."

"What flavor?" Amelia said, "because I really don't want to be something boring like cherry. I'm thinking more of a mango-tangerine combo."

"Sure," Cordelia said, "mango-tango, whatever you want."

"Thang is," Mattie said, butting in, "that Dicky guy wasn't supposed to be selling love potions. It's illegal."

I frowned. "Why?"

Mattie blinked slowly. "Because it's wrong to tamper with people's emotions. You make someone fall in love with you, and they might do just about anythin'—marry you, give you all their money, commit murder."

An unsettling feeling gripped my throat and squeezed. "Commit murder?"

"Yep," Carmen said. "So love potions are illegal."

"Has someone done that before?" I said. "Committed murder because of that?"

"Supposedly," Amelia said. "So that's why it's illegal. Anyway, Dicky Downy is back."

"And the hormones are running wild in Magnolia Cove," Cordelia said.

"Will you be nice?" Amelia fumed. Her fists were tight at her sides.

Cordelia rolled her eyes but said nothing. Carmen took the silence as her cue to cut into the pie. She opened the lid and didn't bother to slice and serve. Instead she dug her fork right on in and popped a chunk into her mouth.

Cordelia and Amelia did the same. I, however, knowing that the upcoming weekend would bring nothing but food, food and more glorious food, abstained from stuffing my face full of the enemy's pie.

Cordelia and Amelia chewed, tipping their heads side to side as they deciphered the dessert.

"It's good," Amelia said, "but not great."

Cordelia chewed a little more. "Yeah, it's good. Could use a little more spice—maybe some nutmeg."

Carmen didn't say anything; instead she kept chewing and forking, popping another piece in her mouth.

"You know," Cordelia said, "you're right, Amelia."

"About what?" she answered, licking pumpkin from her fork.

"About the fact that I've been a real nut buster lately."

"Lately?"

"Don't push it," Cordelia warned.

"Is that an apology?" Amelia said.

Cordelia shrugged. "I could be nicer, is all."

"I'll believe it when I see it," Amelia said.

So would I. I loved Cordelia, but she sure as heck was sarcastic as all get-out. I knew she loved Amelia, but she was pretty hard on our cousin, never cutting her a break.

Amelia stared at the pie. "Like I said, it's missing something. I think it needs a bit more nutmeg." She dropped her fork. Apparently one bite had been enough for her.

Carmen pursed her lips and nodded slightly. "Yep, that's what I think, too. That's why I scrapped that recipe."

We stared at each other. I was the first to speak. "What're you talking about? Scrapped the recipe?"

Carmen tapped the top of the pie with her fork. "This is my recipe. I can tell by the hint of orange in it. It's one I liked, but eventually decided not to pursue because I could never get the spices quite right. It has a touch of star anise, orange zest, nutmeg, cinnamon, allspice and cardamon. It's my recipe all right."

She studied us one by one before finishing with, "The Sweet Witch stole my pumpkin pie recipe. Lori Lou is selling it as her own."

FOUR

"*M*y magical recipe Rolodex was hacked a few weeks ago. At first I thought it was a mistake, that I just imagined it, but now I'm positive."

We sat in the back of Carmen's shop, drinking coffee. Amelia and Cordelia were squeezed into a booth, and I sat in chair. Mattie the Cat lay curled on the floor beside us. She had her eyes closed, but she didn't fool me. That cat wasn't napping; she was zeroing in on everything we said.

"Your magical recipe Rolodex?" I said.

Carmen waved a hand, and what looked like a fiery golden cookbook appeared. She flicked her wrist and the book opened, revealing recipe card after card. They flipped like a book. I don't know why Carmen called it a Rolodex.

But heck, I wasn't going to argue.

Carmen pumped her palm, and the recipes stopped flipping. They landed on a page titled Zingy Pumpkin Pie.

"This is it," Carmen said. "This is the recipe that was stolen. I wasn't sure with the first bite, but after a couple I know it's the one that thief took. You can't replicate those flavors. Why would you try?"

"It does make a good pie," Amelia said. "It's different."

Carmen's mouth coiled into a sad smile. "That's also how I know it's mine." She paused, tapped her mouth and straightened. "Well, they're not going to get away with this. You can't steal a witch's recipe and not expect consequences. You just can't. That's wrong."

She clapped her hands, and the recipe Rolodex disappeared. Carmen gazed out the window of Marshmallow Magic to the Sweet Witch. "One way or another, that witch is going to pay."

∼

"Wow, I have never seen Carmen like that," I said.

"Me neither," Amelia added.

We went back to Familiar Place. Since the great Magnolia Cove Thanksgiving Turkey Hunt was going to start soon, I decided to lock up shop.

After all, the entire town would be consumed with hunting and pecking for frozen turkeys because that was their crazy tradition.

I followed my cousins to the park behind Bubbling Cauldron. It was a meadow that spread behind the courthouse. Magnolia and poplar trees sprinkled the grounds. Far in the corner sat a small pond. It was so pretty. The leaves had all turned at this point. Most of them had fallen except for a few stragglers.

I zipped my jacket to my chin and punched my hands into my pockets. Mattie wound around my legs.

"Don't trip me."

"I'm trying to stay warm," she said. "This place is cold."

"You need a sunbeam," I said.

"Here, you can rest in my arms," Cordelia said.

Amelia and I exchanged confused looks as Mattie jumped into Cordelia's arms and snuggled tight. Never, and I mean never, had we witnessed Cordelia giving any kind of love to an animal. She never even planted sugar on their heads.

By sugar, I mean a kiss.

The entire park had been roped off with brown and green ribbon.

Most of the town surrounded it, waiting patiently for the ribbon to be cut.

"Aren't y'all excited?"

I glanced over my shoulder to see Idie Claire Hawker, town gossip and hairstylist, standing next to me, grinning from ear to ear.

"Excited about the hunt?" I said.

Idie plumped her hair that was teased to heaven. "Yes, it's just so much fun. And with that new baker in town, leaving her pies for us to find, this should be a winner."

"Sure," I said.

Betty Craple appeared over a grassy knoll, flaring to life like a phoenix rising from the ashes.

Her fists were clenched tight and her lips zipped so hard I thought the extra pressure might make her head pop slap off her neck.

"What's going on?" I said when she reached us.

"That woman is causing more mayhem than a prostitute in church."

"Shouldn't prostitutes be allowed in church? They're people, too," Amelia said.

Amelia withered under Betty's glare. "Don't you be back talking me, young lady. These pies are causing all kinds of problems."

"What kind of problem?" I said.

"Just look at those people over there; they're barely staying behind the ribbon."

I glanced at a cluster of townsfolk under a copse of maples. They gripped the ribbon. White knuckles flashed in the sunshine.

"It'll be fine," I said.

Betty scoffed. "Someone's going to get hurt."

I scanned the crowd, and for the briefest of moments I wished Axel was standing beside me. I had loved attending town events with him. It was fun hearing him explain the ins and outs of town dynamics.

Now all I had was Betty crab appling about how her event was ruined because Lori Lou had hijacked it.

Of course, Lori Lou had also stolen Carmen's recipe. According to Carmen, that is.

"You thief!"

Everything stopped. All of us turned. I cringed. Actually I didn't just cringe; my stomach twisted into a pretzel and then plummeted past my feet to the center of the earth.

Carmen stood on the outskirts of the circle, confronting Lori Lou.

"You stole my pumpkin pie recipe and are selling it off as your own!"

Lori clutched her pearls. Her face twisted into a horrified expression. "I would never do anything like that!"

"You did and I'll prove it," Carmen shouted.

Cordelia nudged Betty. "Time to start."

With a light of triumph in her eyes, Betty waddled over to the small platform that doubled as her stage. She tapped the microphone.

"Ladies and gentlemen."

Carmen and Lori Lou parted, but not before my cousin shot the newcomer a hideous glance.

Everyone turned their attention to Betty. I scanned the crowd.

"Everyone's here," I whispered to Amelia.

"Yep. The mayor, all the store owners."

I nodded toward a spot catty-corner from us. "There's moonshine guy, Parker Moody, and even Dicky."

Her eyebrows shot up. "Dicky?"

"You want me to fix y'all up?" Cordelia popped her head between us.

Amelia retreated. "No, why would I want that?"

"I don't know. He's cute, rich, available."

"You don't know he's available," Amelia said.

Cordelia clicked her tongue. "I didn't see a ring."

Mattie blinked from her spot in Cordelia's arms. "Ain't no ring, sugar. Means no wife. He's free for the taking. Though you might not want him."

"He's not a moon pie or a GooGoo Cluster," I said. "He's a person."

Amelia stared at Cordelia. "You're being too nice."

Cordelia shrugged in response.

Amelia prodded. "You hate Dicky."

Cordelia ignored her.

Betty was almost finished. "Mayor, if you'll cut the ribbon, I'll sound the alarm and the twentieth annual Magnolia Cove Turkey Hunt will begin!"

The mayor swiped a hand over his silver hair. Wielding a huge pair of silver shears, he cut the ribbon. Betty brought her fingers to her lips and whistled so high it hurt.

"Ow." I plugged my ears to keep the drums from popping.

"Let the hunt begin," Betty shouted.

And they were off. A couple of hundred people flooded the meadow, sprinting for frozen turkeys.

Frozen turkeys, y'all.

Now if it had been a princess-cut diamond in a platinum band, I would've knocked folks over to find it.

Of course, I would've needed a guy to put the ring on my finger, and Axel was nowhere to be found. I fished my phone from my purse and checked the screen.

No phone calls, same as the last three weeks. Well, no phone calls from him, anyway.

I sighed and dropped it back inside. Amelia shouldered me. "You want to see if we can find a turkey?"

I shrugged. "Sure. As long as we don't get trampled by folks, that is."

"I'll protect y'all," Mattie said, yawning.

"From what? A pack of mice?"

She pawed her whiskers. "Sounds about right."

"I'll come too," Cordelia said.

We traipsed the meadow. A few people already held turkeys and pies high in victory.

"It's always nice to win a turkey the day before Thanksgiving," Amelia said. "Gives a person a sense of accomplishment."

Cordelia opened her mouth and shut it tight.

Amelia fisted a hand to her hip. "What?" she said dramatically. "What were you going to say?"

Cordelia tucked a long strand of blonde hair behind her ear. "I wasn't going to say anything."

"Yes, you were," Amelia stated. "You were going to say something mean. I know you were."

Cordelia sighed and shot me a look full of resignation. "Fine. I was going to say something smart about the fact that I'm sure, yeah, finding a hidden turkey in a bush gives a witch a real sense of accomplishment. It's nothing like creating a spell that clears up your eczema or mends a broken leg."

Amelia pressed her fingers to her forehead. "All I meant was that it's a nice thing. Why do you have to be such a meanie all the time?"

Cordelia inhaled a staggering breath. Y'all, I'm not kidding. She sucked air so loud I could hear the rumble in her throat. She glared at Amelia.

"I'm trying to be nice, get it? Nice. I'm trying to be helpful and kind. It's the freaking holiday of giving thanks, and I'm trying to give, here. I stopped myself from saying it, but you're the one who pushed me to speak. You realize that, right?"

Amelia shrank back. "Okay," she whimpered.

"Sheesh. Can't a person be nice when they want to?"

Amelia punched her hands into her jacket pockets. "Yes. Sorry I questioned you. Let's go find a turkey."

Most of the crowd had veered left, running and chasing the ever elusive hidden bird and pie. I pointed to a small koi pond. "There's a turkey in the bushes back there. Let's go see if someone found it."

"Can I have the gizzard?" Mattie said.

My gaze darted to her. "You want the gizzard raw?"

"No, sugar bear. I want y'all to cook it up good and crispy and then place it delicate like in my bowl."

"Sounds like a plan."

We rounded the bushes. "I think Betty stuck it behind that tree."

Mattie sprang from Cordelia's arms. "What's that smell?"

The cat bounded into the trees, skirting behind a four-foot-wide trunk.

"What smell?" I said.

"Blood," Mattie said. "I smell blood."

"I don't smell blood," Amelia said.

Cordelia shot me a hard look. I knew she wanted to say something smart, was dying to, so I did it for her.

"Cats have better smell than we do, Amelia. If Mattie's picked up the scent of blood, it's true." I walked around a tree. "Where's the blood coming from?"

Mattie's voice drifted to me from a couple of trees away. "It's coming from right here."

The three of us rounded the oaks, coming to a stop at Mattie's feet. Amelia screamed.

"Looks like we found the last turkey," Cordelia said.

Splayed out beside a frozen Butterball was the lifeless body of Lori Lou Fick. The giant ribbon-cutting scissors were punched squarely through her throat. Lori Lou's lifeless eyes stared at the blue sky as she clutched a turkey with a clawlike grip.

Amelia pulled her fingers from her lips. "Gosh. I guess that wasn't an accident, was it?"

Cordelia shook her head. "Nope. Ladies, looks like we've got a Thanksgiving murder on our hands."

Great. Just when I was hoping that we'd have a quiet holiday, it looked like my dreams were getting thrown out the door and sucked into a witch-nado.

"You thank someone didn't like her pie?" Mattie said.

I shook my head. "No. I think someone wanted her dead."

FIVE

*G*arrick Young, the town sheriff and Cordelia's boyfriend, swooped in and cordoned off the body.

Garrick was tall and lean, and wore a thick brown belt on his low-slung jeans. He also wore the official uniform of the Magnolia Cove Police—a wide-brimmed fedora and long leather duster.

Don't ask me why, but that's what the police wore. I think they wanted to pretend they were Hugh Jackman in *Van Helsing.*

"So y'all didn't see anything?" Garrick said, his brown eyes lighting on me, my cousins and Mattie the Cat.

"Not a thing," Cordelia said. "We came across her when we were looking for a turkey."

Garrick pinched his hat's brim and slid his fingers across it. "I heard Carmen Craple and Lori Lou got into it right before the hunt."

"Oh yes," Amelia offered. "Carmen accused Lori Lou of stealing her pumpkin pie recipe. Carmen's been ticked because the Sweet Witch is taking all her customers."

"Really?" Garrick said with a heavy dose of police interest.

I shot Amelia a scathing look. Her gaze darted to me; then she gulped loudly. "I mean, I think Carmen was ticked. You know, now that I recall, I've never really seen our cousin angry." She turned to us. "Have y'all?"

"No. Nope," we said.

He tapped his fingers against his hips. "Good try. I'll be talking to her. Don't worry, seems like several folks were ticked at Lori Lou."

"Why?" I said, hoping that Garrick would divulge police business mainly because I didn't want to see Carmen in trouble. I mean, I know my cousin was royally annoyed by Lori Lou, but not enough to kill.

Right?

Garrick laughed. "Now what in tarnation makes you think I'm going to be sharing that?"

"Our good looks?" I said cheerfully.

"Think again. Now y'all run along. I'm sure you've got lots of preparing to do for dinner tomorrow."

We stalked back across the meadow. A crowd had gathered on the outskirts of the yellow police tape. I saw Becky Ray, Lori Lou's sister, on the edge of the tape. My chest seized.

I mean, I was pretty sure it was Becky Ray. She was the only person wearing a chef's hat when she should've been wearing normal, everyday clothing in strong fall colors.

The poor woman's sister was dead. *Dead*. Thanksgiving was tomorrow. It was just horrible.

Without thinking, I quickly crossed the field and threw my hands around her neck.

Becky Ray was stiff as a board. However, she wasn't light as a feather, if you know what I mean. "I'm so sorry about your sister."

I released my grip. Becky wiped tears away with the heel of her hand. "My only sister."

"Listen, I don't know what you're doing tomorrow, but if you want to, come to our house for dinner. I know it won't be the same, but you can't be alone."

"I have Collinsworth," she said. Becky had a really deep voice, almost gravelly. She was also thickly built, reminding me of a boxer or an ultimate fighting champion.

"We'd love to have you both."

Becky Ray frowned but didn't say anything other than, "Thank you."

I rejoined my cousins and explained about inviting Becky Ray to dinner. Both of them thought it was the right thing to do. As we were walking back, I realized I'd forgotten to turn off the lights in Familiar Place.

"I've got to run by the store and shut off the lights. Y'all going straight home?"

Amelia scoffed. "Sure as heck we are. It's Thanksgiving Eve. Betty'll be in a tizzy about the meal, plus the fact that she has to make the chicken poulet."

"Chicken poulet?" I said. "What's that?"

Cordelia rolled her eyes. "It puts Betty in an ugly mood every year, is what it is."

"That explains it," I said.

"What Cordelia means to say is that it's the most amazing dish ever. It's dressing and chicken and milk and eggs. Basically it's chicken cooked in dressing but the recipe is foolproof—you can't screw it up. The dressing won't be too dry and it won't be flavorless because you use good old Pepperidge Farm straight from the bag. But because it's the only dressing-like thing she makes on Thanksgiving, it always freaks her out and she gets all wound up. It's horrible."

Cordelia nodded. "That sounds about right."

"And Axel loves it," Amelia said, smiling. She stopped, closed her eyelids tight. "I'm sorry. I didn't mean..."

I raised my palm. "It's okay. He exists. He existed. We can talk about him."

"But he ripped out your heart and threw it on the ground," Amelia said in her exuberantly optimistic way that made it hard for me to want to witch-slap her.

"Amelia," Cordelia warned.

Amelia's eyes widened. "I'm sorry, did I say something wrong?"

"Almost everything," Cordelia said.

"It's okay, really. It's fine. I'm okay. Getting by day by day."

"Has he called?" Amelia said.

Cordelia yanked her by the arm. "Let's go. We can talk to Pepper about this another time—not right after witnessing Lori Lou scissored to death."

"Ew, why'd you have to put it like that?" Amelia said. "That's so gross."

Cordelia waved. "We'll see you at the house." She dragged our cousin down the street. I could still hear Amelia protesting as they disappeared onto the next block.

Mattie blinked at me from the ground. "Well, sugar bear, come on. Let's go shut off those lights."

I raked my fingers through my hair, snagging on a knot along the way. "You sure you don't want to go home?"

"Nah. I love being outside this time of year."

We reached Familiar Place a few minutes later. I unlocked the door with the golden key my Uncle Donovan had left me and pushed the handle. I worked quickly, starting in the back and snapping off the lights one by one.

The kittens and puppies tried to protest.

"Hey, stay awhile!"

"Don't turn off that light! We want to party!"

But I ignored them. I flipped the last switch and greeted Mattie on the doorstep. "All done."

I locked the door and turned to head back home when something snagged my attention. I bent over, peering across the street. I'm pretty sure I looked like a peeping Pepper. Good thing the rest of town was busy at the murder scene.

"What is it, sugar bear?" Mattie said.

"The lights are on at the Sweet Witch."

The cat glanced over. "They sure are. Is that someone walking around in there?"

I shot Mattie a conspiratorial look. "You thinking what I'm thinking?"

"That the murderer is in that there shop right now stealing whatever it was they didn't get off Lori Lou's body? Yep."

I scooped Mattie into my arms. "Let's go around back."

I walked the long sidewalk, keeping an eye on the shop the entire time. Thoughts raced through my head.

Please don't let it be Carmen in there.

There was no way my cousin would kill someone, but she had pitched a near hissy-going-on-conniption fit at the park. Worse, the entire town witnessed it. Witnessed my cool cousin about to pull Lori Lou's hair straight from her Aqua Netted roots.

I was so full of angst my stomach knotted. I could feel my insides turning to water and knew my intestines would be cramping anytime soon. I needed to get that crap under control.

A good Southern gal always has her cool down pat. I needed to be cool, even if it meant getting ready to karate chop a murderer.

Ugh. Too bad I didn't know how to karate chop. Maybe I could flail my arms around and look fierce.

Sure. That would work.

Probably not.

I reached the back door, but not before tripping over a pile of black trash bags. "What in the world? I almost broke my neck on these." For good measure I kicked them to the side and settled Mattie on the ground. The cat stretched and pawed the knob. "I got a plan."

"Great," I whispered. "What is it?"

"I'll run in, jump on whoever's in there and scratch their eyes out."

I cringed. It was definitely better than my plan and also more gruesome. "Okay, maybe we tone it down. Why don't you run and jump on their head to blind them. Meanwhile I'll come in from behind with a karate chop to the kidney. That way we can immobilize whoever it is."

Mattie extended her claws on the door. "Sounds good. Open this baby."

I glanced up and noticed a padlock on the outside had been broken clean in two. My stomach knotted. Whoever was inside had definitely done so using deviant methods.

"Be careful," I warned Mattie.

"Will do, sugar bear."

My fingers shook as I reached for the knob. This was one of those times that I wished Axel was with me.

Can it, Pepper. The man's not coming back. You just need to tighten your panties and get the heck over it. Stop being a whiny baby.

I turned the knob. It gave with ease. I cracked the door, and Mattie scampered it, meowing and spitting.

Crap. If I'd have known it was all-out war, I would've called Betty for some gear.

I followed quickly, but Mattie hightailed it faster than I could keep up. Next thing I knew, she was hissing, someone else was yelling and I was standing in the kitchen of the Sweet Witch.

"I got him," Mattie screeched.

I ran from the kitchen to the display room and saw Mattie sitting atop a clearly confused Collinsworth.

"What in the world? Why are you on my head?"

I couldn't help but laugh at the picture of a cat, paws clapped around the bunny's eyes. With a cat and bunny, I was wondering if a dish was going to run away with a spoon.

Mattie jumped down. Collinsworth straightened his waistcoat and cleared his throat. "Might I ask what in God's name are you doing breaking and entering this store?"

"I might ask you the same thing," I said, crossing my arms. "The padlock was broken and here you are. Aren't you supposed to be Lori Lou's helper animal? Yet you're scavenging around with only one light on. It looks very suspicious."

Tears filled Collinsworth's eyes. "I know about Lori Lou. I was at the turkey hunt. We got separated and then, then—" He burst into tears.

"She got herself murdered," Mattie finished for him.

"Yes." Collinsworth rubbed his eyes. "I'm sorry. I came back to get something of hers. Something I could remember her by." He lifted a silk handkerchief. "It was her favorite. Please. I wasn't doing anything wrong. I loved Lori Lou. I want the police to find her killer."

I smirked, still undecided about whether or not I believed him. But then the bunny glanced up at me with eyes full of tears and my heart melted—even if he did have a horribly fake British accent.

"Why didn't you wait until Becky Ray opened tomorrow?" I said.

"Because I didn't know if Becky would open. Besides, Becky hates me. Detests me. She thinks I'm too smart for my own waistcoat."

"She's probably right," Mattie said. She yawned and glanced at me. "Come on, Pepper. Let's go."

"Wait," he said, hopping forward. "I don't have anywhere to go. I can't return to my house with Lori Lou. What if the murderer shows up and kills me, too?"

I nibbled the inside of my lip. "I don't know. We have a pretty full house."

I know it was Thanksgiving, but I mean, this rabbit had a place to go, I was pretty sure. Surely Becky Ray didn't hate him. He was probably being dramatic, playing a sympathy card for some reason.

Collinsworth hopped in front of me, blocking my path. "Please. You must help me."

"Why?" I said.

Don't ask me why I didn't feel the need to help him. Maybe it was because I'd already offered Becky Ray to come to the house. Maybe it was because I didn't buy his story that Becky Ray didn't like him. Why would she have allowed a rabbit in the store if she didn't like him? Made no sense to me.

But all my doubts vanished when Collinsworth stepped forward and said, "Please. You must help me. My life is in danger."

SIX

*M*attie gave me a good once-over. "Whatever you want to do. I'm leaving this decision up to you, Pepper."

I sucked my teeth. "Okay, rabbit. Why is your life in danger?"

He hopped forward. His little fat rabbit legs quivered. "Don't you see? Whoever killed Lori Lou may kill me next."

"Why?"

"Because...I don't know, but I'm sure there's a good reason for it. I'm sure they'll want to kill me. I'm a poor, defenseless bunny rabbit. I wouldn't survive out there in the cold, harsh world by myself. Look at me? I'm one shot away from rabbit stew."

Mattie licked her mouth. "Sounds yummy."

I shot her a dark look. She rolled her green eyes but said nothing. It *was* Thanksgiving and I was in the spirit of giving, after all. If I couldn't offer a defenseless rabbit who probably dropped turds after every step a place to sleep for one night, then I was a harsh, evil person.

I almost laughed maniacally to prove it. Instead I deflated. My shoulders slouched as I exhaled a deep shot of air.

"Okay, rabbit. You can stay with us tonight. But you've got to find a place to live."

"Thank you." He shuffled back. "Now let me grab my hat and we'll be on our way."

"Hat?" Mattie said.

I gently pressed her side, nudging the cat to the rear of the building. Collinsworth reappeared with his hat. It was a straw barber-shop-quartet style getup. He looked completely ridiculous.

"Okay, Benjamin Bunny," I said, referencing a character from the *Peter Rabbit* books.

"I'm Collinsworth the Rabbit."

"So you keep telling me." I shut the back door and glanced at the broken lock. "You don't have a key?"

"No. I used an old magic trick to get in."

"What sort of magic trick?"

He explained as we walked home. "I used to be a magician's rabbit, and one of the tricks he used to perform was the old sawing-a-person-in-half routine. He had a magic saw. The thing wouldn't cut flesh, but it would slice up metal easily. I have the saw, and I can jump pretty high."

"Where's it now?"

"Oh, I left it behind some crates. I didn't think anyone would need it."

Right. No one would need or want a saw that broke through metal but didn't injure flesh. Note to self: return to pick up said incredibly dangerous saw in the near future.

Right when I was thinking that, Mattie shot me a look that said she was thinking the same thing. Collinsworth half hopped, half walked beside us.

A spark of tenderness lit inside me at seeing the little furry guy ambling along.

"Don't worry, Collinsworth," I said, "we'll get to the bottom of this."

Mattie tapped me with her tail. "We will?"

"Sure we will. But right now let's go enjoy a quiet Thanksgiving Eve at home. Maybe by the time we arrive, Betty will have settled down in her giant muumuu with a cup of hot chocolate in her hands."

No deal.

When we reached the house, Betty was strolling about the lawn, weaving through a throng of furniture that should've been inside but was now sitting outside on yellowing November fescue.

"What are you doing?" I said.

"Cleaning house," Betty said. She stared at the pile of things—an end table, a wicker chair, some kitchen towels and a nightstand. She nodded in approval and clapped her hands. A sign appeared, posted into the grass.

"Free?" I said, unsure what was going on. "You're giving these things away?"

Betty snorted. "Kid, it's the season for giving and I'm giving."

"It's the season of Thanksgiving. The season of giving thanks, not doling out Christmas presents like an STD on steroids."

Betty glared at me. Amelia appeared on the porch. "What in the world?"

My cousin raced down the steps and yanked an end table from its perch. "This is mine. Mine. It goes in my room. What's it doing out here?"

"It's causing clutter," Betty said. "I'm giving it away."

Amelia dragged it toward the house. "No, you're not. I'm keeping this."

Betty clenched her teeth. Uh-oh. This was going to be a fight. Like a serious witchy battle on the night before a holiday.

"You can have something of mine," I said. "Don't take her table. Take something from my room."

Betty pulled her pipe from her pocket and shoved it in her mouth. She didn't bother packing it or even lighting it. The thing was already smoking by the time it hit her teeth.

I stared at her clothes. "Was that lit inside your pocket this whole time?"

"What's it to you?" She thumbed toward the rabbit. "Who's this?"

I cleared my throat. Clearly first impressions had been tossed out the window. "This is Collinsworth. He belonged to Lori Lou. He's afraid someone may want to harm him."

"Oh, Lori was harboring secrets, was she?" Betty said.

"Um, no. She was just very popular," Collinsworth said.

Betty's eyebrows ratcheted up a notch. "So popular she stole my niece's pumpkin pie recipe?"

Collinsworth palmed his hat nervously. "I don't know anything about recipe stealing. All I know is that she made people happy." He glanced around. "Can we go inside? It's very cold out here."

I steered him by the shoulder toward the door. Jenny the guard-vine uncoiled and sniffed Collinsworth from head to cottontail.

Once that was complete, we scooted inside. Betty came with us but stopped and stared at the furniture. Knowing she was trying to figure out what else to set outside in her weirdly strange new Thanksgiving tradition, I glanced around the room for a distraction.

"Whoa. Is that the pie from the Sweet Witch?"

An open box displaying a pecan pie sat atop the dining table. The box was slightly rumpled and the pie itself looked like it had fallen upside down but had been righted. On one side all the pecans were pushed up against the edge while the other side was empty.

The chocolate bat was half eaten.

I crossed to it. "Is that? Is that the pie we threw in the trash?"

Betty's lower lip trembled. "Maybe."

Vomit edged up the back of my throat. I seriously wanted to hurl. "Why is it out of the trash and sitting on the table?"

"I got hungry," Betty said glumly. "Stress makes me eat."

"What stress?"

She threw up her hands. "The fiasco at the park. My Thanksgiving Turkey Hunt was ruined by that woman who hid pies and then up and died right there. This town's had enough problems lately without some hussy getting murdered right before the holiday."

"First of all—Collinsworth," I said, pointing to him.

Betty rolled her eyes and spat out a not-so-believable, "Sorry. Lori Lou wasn't a hussy. At least not that I was aware of."

"Secondly," I said, "that pie was in the trash. That's disgusting. You'll probably get worms and have to go to the vet."

"Watch it," Mattie said.

"No offense. There's nothing wrong with vets, but that's gross."

"Mind your own business," Betty said. "I've had a rough day. If I want to eat good trash, then I'll eat it."

"Okay then. Well, before you decide to put any more things outside, I'm going upstairs to acquaint Collinsworth with Hugo."

"Who, may I ask, is Hugo?" the rabbit said as we climbed the stairs.

"My pet dragon."

He stopped. "P-p-pet d-d-dragon?"

I nodded. "Yes." I glanced at the rabbit. His knees were shaking something fierce. "Don't worry. He won't eat you."

"Oh, good."

"At least I don't think so."

When I opened the door, Hugo greeted me with a thump of his tail. He uncoiled from his spot on the floor and trotted over to greet me. His tongue lolled to one side as I gave him a good pat.

"Hugo, meet Collinsworth the Rabbit."

Hugo cocked his head. The dragon, who was about the size of a hope chest, lumbered over to the rabbit and gave a good sniff.

Collinsworth squeaked. Hugo playfully nipped his head, and the rabbit almost fainted.

"Hugo, he's not food. He's here as our guest." I shucked off my shoes and slumped to the bed. "Listen, y'all, settle down. I'll go see what's for dinner. I'll be back in a bit." I pointed a finger at them. "Nobody eats anybody else. Mattie, you're in charge."

"Aye, aye, sugar." She bounded to the window seat and curled up. I checked my phone before letting it fall to the quilt.

"No calls?" Mattie said.

"None." My face crumpled. "I don't even know why I bother looking."

"He'll call one day, Pepper. He will. I know that man loves you."

I scoffed. "He's got a hysterical way of showing it. Insane, even."

"He's just scared."

"Are we discussing a man of the male persuasion?" Collinsworth said.

"Was the fact that we used the word 'he' a dead giveaway?" Mattie said.

"Be nice," I warned. "Yes, we're talking about a man."

Collinsworth jumped on my bed. I grimaced. I really, really hoped he didn't squirt turds on it.

He dropped his hat on my pillow. "I might be of some assistance."

I stifled a laugh. "Listen, I don't think sending you as a candy gram to Axel will make him come back."

Collinsworth shrugged. "You never know. Still, if you change your mind, let me know."

I slipped downstairs to see what Betty had made for supper.

"All we're having is turnip greens and cornbread," she said before I could ask. "The real meal is tomorrow."

I slumped to the table. Amelia and Cordelia were already seated. Cordelia flashed me a bright smile.

"You look so pretty tonight, Pepper."

I did a double take. Was she on drugs? I leaned over until my reflection greeted me from a wall mirror. The dark circles tattooed under my eyes didn't look to be going anywhere, and my hair hung limply around my face. It was in serious need of a washing.

"Are you okay?" I said to Cordelia.

"I'm great. Fantastic," she said, a wide grin spreading across her face.

Amelia shook her head and widened her eyes as if to say, *Cordelia has lost her cotton-pickin' mind.*

Betty joined us at the table. She pulled back her chair and mumbled, "You think that's enough stuff outside?"

"Yes," Amelia and I said at once.

Cordelia's phone chimed. She picked it from the table and thumbed the Accept button.

"Hey," she said in a smoky voice. Long pause. "Are you sure? You have to? But it's Thanksgiving." Another pause. "I just don't believe that. Okay. I understand."

She hung up.

"What is it?" I said.

Tears filled Cordelia's eyes. She bit her bottom lip. "That was Garrick. He's made an arrest in the Lori Lou case."

"Who?" I said, praying my cousin wasn't going to say the name I was afraid she would.

"Carmen. He's arrested Carmen. Said the evidence is overwhelming."

The four of us exchanged a long look. Betty smacked her lips. "Think she'll need a lamp in jail? I've got one I can give her."

I smacked my forehead. "Sure you don't just want to drop off the entire house at the jail?"

Betty jabbed the air with her fork. "Don't tempt me."

Amelia grabbed my arm. "Pepper, we've got to help Carmen. She's innocent. We all know that."

"Well, girls," Betty said, adjusting her glasses, "looks like we're in for one busy Thanksgiving."

"How's that?" I said.

"First thing tomorrow morning, we're going to break your cousin out of jail."

SEVEN

We didn't wake up and break Carmen out of jail. Betty had only been joking, though I wouldn't have put it past Amelia and Cordelia because they were pretty upset.

First thing the next morning, Betty, Amelia, Cordelia, Collinsworth and myself did go to the station to visit Carmen. Betty took a hummingbird cake. I was pretty sure that my grandmother had considered baking a nail file in it.

Garrick checked. "There isn't a file in that cake, is there?"

Betty pounded her fists to her hips. "No, and if you want to taste it, you can. Happy Thanksgiving to you."

Garrick scraped his fingers down his face. "Carmen's over here."

He escorted us to the cell where Carmen sat on a thin cot. She saw us and raced to the bars.

"My lawyer's coming later today."

"Who is it?" Betty said.

"Farinas Harrell," Carmen said.

Amelia sucked air. "Farinas? Like the Farinas who made an entire town bankrupt when they wrongly accused a witch of ladling out potions?"

Carmen eyed Garrick. "That's the one. She'll be here right after dinner. Y'all should meet her."

"We brought you cake," Cordelia said.

"Thank you. Maybe I'll have some for breakfast, but I don't have much of an appetite."

We said our goodbyes and left the cake. Cordelia shot Garrick a look that made him stare at the floor and rub his neck.

Ew. I guess things weren't so hot between them since he'd arrested our cousin. To be honest, I'd be ticked, too.

We walked downtown, which was surprisingly busy for a holiday morning. You'd have thought that most witches and wizards would be sleeping in, but not today.

We passed Idie Claire Hawker's beauty shop, Spells and Shears. Idie stepped out the door, onto the sidewalk. She wrapped her orange scarf around her neck, took one look at us and smiled widely.

"Y'all, I am giving free haircuts tomorrow. Free haircuts." She wrapped her hands around my arms. "Pepper, you know I've been dying to play with yours."

And you know I don't want it teased to high heaven.

I smiled widely. "Thanks, Idie. I'll think about it."

Idie didn't miss a beat. She grinned at Betty. "And your curls could use a trim, too, Miss Craple."

Betty snorted. "You know good and well I get my hair set once a week, Idie. I'm not coming in for a trim."

Idie didn't let that stop her. She then turned to Collinsworth. "And does someone need a shave?"

The rabbit hopped behind my legs. "I most certainly do not need any sort of shear-related trim, thank you very much. I am fine."

Idie hitched a shoulder and smiled vacantly. "Well, anyway, happy Thanksgiving, y'all."

"Happy Thanksgiving," I murmured.

We kept on until we reached Castin' Iron, the store that creates and sells the long cast-iron skillets all the witches in town ride. The owners, Harry and Theodora, carted merchandise onto the sidewalk.

"Happy Thanksgiving," Theodora said. "Need a new skillet? We're having a sale. Take one for free and you can have another."

I stopped. "You're giving them away?"

She wrapped her long white hair over one shoulder. "Oh yes, we're running out of room inside."

"Stop it!" Harry yelled. "We're giving them away because we want to, not because we're running out of room."

Theodora rolled her eyes. "It's just something to say, Harry. Mind your own beeswax and keep moving skillets."

Harry dropped a riding skillet to the sidewalk with a humph. "I won't be moving any more. I'm tired and hungry. Make me my breakfast, woman."

Theodora shook her head. "Men are so helpless unless a woman isn't around. Then they can do everything for themselves."

I linked gazes with Cordelia and laughed. It did seem true and funny. Yet there was something off about the whole thing. Why would they give their wares away?

We wished the couple goodbye and moved on.

I sidled up to Amelia. "Something strange is happening."

Her mouth puckered to a perfect bow. "Like what do you mean?"

I lowered my voice. "Don't you think everyone's acting weird? First, Cordelia starts being nice to you, then Betty decides to give away half the house and now folks are handing out things they'd never give for free."

Amelia nibbled the inside of her lip. "Yeah, I guess something strange is happening. But what?"

"I don't know." I shook my hair out. "Maybe it's nothing. Maybe I'm overreacting. Oh!" I strode to Betty. "I need to stop by my store and feed the animals. Let them wake up for a while since I'm not open. I'll meet you back at the house."

Betty eyed me. "Better hurry, kid. We've got a whole slew of folks showing up at one. I need all the hands I can get to finish up dinner."

I squeezed her shoulder. "I promise, I'll be there quick as I can."

"I'll stay with you," Collinsworth chirped. "I'm afraid your dragon will eat me if I return there alone."

"Okay."

The rabbit followed me to Familiar Place. I'd almost reached the store when the squealing of tires caught my attention.

A black sedan with dark tinted windows peeled away from the alley behind the Sweet Witch. When I say peeled away, what I mean is the car was burning rubber. Like seriously burning rubber as if they'd just encountered ebola and the driver was scared to death.

I was carrying my phone and snapped a picture of the plate before it disappeared from sight. "That's weird."

"Hmm," Collinsworth said distractedly.

Something smelled funny in the air, and it wasn't the track marks the vehicle left on the asphalt. "Collinsworth, who were those men?"

"What men?"

"The ones who drove away?"

"I don't know what you're talking about."

I pointed across the street. "And what do you think I'll find if we go investigate the shop? Looks like Becky Ray didn't open this morning."

He hitched a furry shoulder. "I can't say. Perhaps you should ask the owner of Magical Moonshine. It looks like he's open."

He was. I could see Parker Moody in the store. "Come on."

"Where?"

"We're going to talk to Parker."

Collinsworth backed up. "That monster? He entered the store and yelled at Lori Lou. I thought he might throw something, harm someone. He's horrible. I can't face him again."

Before the rabbit could keep arguing and give me a whooper of a migraine, I scooped him up and crossed the street.

"Let me go. You can't drag me wherever you want. I have rights."

I clutched his feet so he'd stop kicking. "Listen, rabbit. You're the one who came to me needing help. You said someone may try to kill you. Those men didn't look like they were from around here. Now, they were either in the back of the moonshine joint or the bakery. You say you've never seen them and don't know who they are. Well, I'm putting that to the test."

I couldn't place my finger on it, but I was certain this little furry critter was keeping secrets. He went back to the store for a handkerchief? Thought someone might kill him? Says Becky Ray hates him?

Hog-freaking-wash. No doubt about it.

With the little beast still struggling, I hipped open the door of Magical Moonshine. Parker Moody stood behind the counter wiping down the surface.

"Happy Thanksgiving," he said.

I gently lowered Collinsworth to the floor, dusted my hands and held back a sneeze. Apparently I was allergic to rabbit dander. Go figure.

"Happy Thanksgiving," I said.

"Care to try a taste of apple pie moonshine?"

I wove my way around crates and boxes topped with glass mason jars filled with clear liquid of all different colors—green, amber, yellow, lavender, orange.

I reached the counter. Parker Moody smiled widely. He had clipped brown hair that was graying on the sides. Bright blue eyes twinkled at me, and strong forearms were positioned wide on the counter. The gold band of his wedding ring glinted in the morning sun.

"You're open on Thanksgiving?" I said.

He nodded. "There'll be a rush in a few minutes. I've learned staying open for a few hours like today is worth it." He extended a hand. "Parker Moody."

"Pepper Dunn."

"You own Familiar Place."

I grinned. "Right."

He pulled a jar of green liquid to him and filled a shot glass half-full. "I've been meaning to bring my daughter in. She's twelve."

I clicked my tongue appreciatively. "Just the right age for her first familiar. I'd love to help her find the perfect animal. Come by anytime."

He pushed the shot glass across the counter. "Free tastings. If you like green apples, you'll love that. Green apple moonshine."

I lifted the glass into the light. It was a delicious looking Jolly Rancher green. My stomach rumbled with delight.

I ratcheted an eyebrow. "What does it do?"

He shifted his weight. "You mean, why's it magical?"

"Yeah."

He slid another shot glass over, filled it with a pale amber liquid. "It does different things. Some witches use the moonshine in spells or potions. Others use it to calm their nerves so they can concentrate on their spells. But most"—his blue eyes sparked with mischief—"use it to feel their power better."

"And get a buzz?"

He nodded to the light brown liquid. "This one's pumpkin pie. Try it."

"I didn't come here to get drunk."

He shrugged in response. I lifted the green apple to my lips and let the liquid slide down my throat. It was smooth—nothing like the burn I'd expected. After a few seconds the strangest thing happened. I felt my magic stir, like it had simply been waiting for me to use it. Like it was a coiled cobra, ready to strike.

"Whew, that's good. Almost too good." My gaze scanned the shelves. "Do you make all these?"

"Sure do."

I walked around and picked up a light pink one labeled Cotton Candy. "Can I try this?"

From behind me, Collinsworth cleared his throat. I shot him a death glare.

"Sure," Parker said. He opened a bottle and poured a finger.

I crossed back to the counter and stopped. "It was terrible about that Lori Lou being murdered."

Parker twisted the cap back on and stopped, stared at me. "Sure was."

I raised the glass and brought it to my lips. "She really ticked off a lot of folks."

"She ticked me off. Always placing her garbage outside by my door. I told her to stop doing that. Told her repeatedly, but she didn't. I couldn't get into my shop because of it."

Garbage. I'd seen several bags outside her back door last night when I'd gone in and found Collinsworth.

"Didn't she have a dumpster?"

He nodded. "Out back. We all do. But she didn't use it."

I didn't bother trying the cotton candy moonshine. Instead I bought it outright and left, hoisting Collinsworth onto my hip as I barreled out the door.

"Whoa, hold on. I'm only a rabbit. I do break."

I raced around back. The garbage bags that I'd kicked the night before were gone. Vanished. The trash truck didn't run on holidays. Everyone knew that. Yes, I know I live in a magical town full of witches, but there was still trash pickup day.

Y'all, some things just don't change whether you're in the magical world or the regular one.

"Collinsworth, what was in those trash bags?"

The rabbit said nothing.

"What was in them?"

"I don't...I don't know."

"You do too know. Why aren't you telling me?"

"I don't know anything about it. Or them. Nothing."

I tapped my booted toe on the ground. "Fine. You don't know anything about the garbage; you don't know anything about who might've wanted to kill Lori Lou, the one person you loved in life. Fine. I'll go to Garrick right now and tell him that you're withholding evidence." I touched my nose to his and glared at the rabbit. "Do you know what the police do to rabbits who withhold evidence?"

"N-n-no. What?" he said quietly.

"They fricassee them. Turn them into stew."

Collinsworth gasped.

Yes, I know it wasn't nice of me to suggest the rabbit would be eaten. I was only bluffing. For those of y'all who wouldn't harm Thumper even though Thumper clearly knew a crapload more than

49

he was telling, don't worry. Your precious baby wasn't going to be anyone's next meal.

"Okay," Collinsworth said.

"Okay what?"

He sighed. "Lori Lou was selling potions out the back door."

I quirked a brow. "What sort of potions?"

Collinsworth kneaded his hands. He gulped loudly. "Love potions. She was selling illegal love potions. And it got her killed."

EIGHT

J stood in Garrick's office. My fist slammed his desk. No, it wasn't pretty. I banged my fist while Garrick eyed me like he was two steps away from throwing a pair of handcuffs on me.

"Carmen didn't kill Lori Lou. The rabbit told me she was selling love potions illegally."

Garrick eyed Collinsworth. "The rabbit?"

"He talks." I nudged the bunny with my toe. "Speak for the man."

"Oh yes, I'm fluent in three languages—English, French and American."

Garrick hid a smile behind his hand.

I pressed my palms flat and leaned over. "Look, I know it sounds crazy, but she was selling love potions."

"Proof?" Garrick said.

My stomach clenched. "Yeah, I'm kind of short on that."

"Then I can't help you." Garrick dropped his feet from the desk and rose. "Listen, Pepper, I know you want to help your cousin, but the best way you can do that is to stay out of it. I know you liked to play investigator with Axel and you miss him. We all do, but this is official police business."

I bristled like a scared cat. "I didn't play investigator with Axel."

Garrick shot me a pointed look.

I raised my palms in surrender. "Okay, maybe I did a little. My relationship with Axel is none of your business."

"I agree. Now get out of here."

"I got a picture of the car that screamed down Bubbling Cauldron. Don't you even want to run the plate, see where it takes you?"

Garrick shook his head. "I'm working a murder case, not a drug one. There's no evidence of it. None. I've got my suspect locked up."

"Oh yeah? What evidence do you have?"

He eyed me coldly. "That's confidential."

I waved my phone in his face. "I'll go to Farinas with this. A lot of bad press can come to this town."

Garrick's face crimsoned. "*You've* caused a lot of bad press in this town," he exploded. "May I remind you that it was your fault the time watch broke and we almost had to suffer through Halloween every day of the year?"

I cringed. "I apologized for that."

"Get out," he demanded. "Get out now. And before you even consider going to Farinas Harrell"—he glanced out his office and shut the door—"between you and me."

My heart leaped. "Between us."

He wagged a finger at me. "If I hear that you or your bunny mouthed one word of this, I swear I'll toss you in a cell."

I crossed my heart. "Promise."

"You swear? Not even your cousins. Not Betty. No one."

"No one." My stomach was a bundle of butterflies. What was Garrick going to tell me?

"Carmen's fingerprints were all over those scissors."

"No." My hand flew to my mouth.

"Yes. So before you start spouting off about there being love potions traded in town, you think about that."

"But she was—she was framed, Garrick. Can't you see that?"

He slumped back in his chair, raised his cowboy-booted feet to the desk. He picked up a stress ball and tossed it from hand to hand. "I've got to do what the clues say. The evidence is overwhelming. I'll tell you one more time—overwhelming. Don't run around and screw it up."

"I wasn't planning on it."

He shot me a dark look.

"Well, I'm not now."

"Better," he said. "Now go enjoy your Thanksgiving. I'll see you at the house this afternoon."

Oh crap! I'd totally forgotten I promised Betty I'd help finish the cooking. I grabbed Collinsworth and waved goodbye.

"See you then!"

I hustled from the station. For once I wished I knew how to fly. I practically ran the entire way home. As I passed cottages, I noticed that other folks had placed furniture on their grass like Betty. Their signs also advertised that the furniture was free.

What in heck's bells was going on?

No time to wonder about it, because Thanksgiving dinner was less than three hours away and I had a crapload of stuff to do—I was just sure of it.

I dropped Collinsworth inside and ran to the kitchen. Betty and my cousins stood at various counters wearing aprons. They were each covered in flour.

I raised the brown bag Parker Moody had given me. "I brought the moonshine!"

"Great," Betty huffed, "'cause we're going to need it to get through this holiday without Carmen. Pepper, put on an apron. Cordelia will tell you what to do."

I did as I was told and stepped beside my cousin who was opening cans of cream of mushroom soup. She slid one toward me.

"That one goes in the green beans."

I dropped it in and stirred. We worked in silence for a couple of hours. I would drop whatever ingredient into a bowl Cordelia shoved my way, stir and mix the contents until they were combined, or at least combined enough that it looked presentable without baking. Then it went either into the oven or atop the fire in the hearth, wherever there was room. We worked like a sweatshop assembly line.

Finally Betty pulled out the turkey. She settled it on the counter, lowered her oven-mitted hands and sighed.

"Now that is one beautiful bird."

I peeked over her shoulder at the splendor. Crisp, golden-brown skin covered the bird from breast to tail. The aroma drifting in the air made my nose tickle. I licked my lips. My stomach clenched in hunger.

"I'm starving." I glanced at my watch. "When is everyone arriving?"

Betty whisked the bird into the small dining room. "Should be any time now."

I wiped my arm over a sheen of sweat on my forehead. "I'm going to wash up."

I pulled the apron over my neck and pegged it in the kitchen. I took the stairs to my bedroom two at a time and entered to find Hugo's jaws opened and Collinsworth's head stuck in his mouth.

"No! Don't eat him! You can't eat him."

Hugo jumped, startled, and knocked over a lamp. The rabbit scampered to my bed and shivered.

The dragon shot me a gaze full of sadness and dropped his head in submission. I gave him a gentle pat. "What's going on?"

"I was showing that evil animal-eating dragon how we performed magic tricks with the magician."

I crossed my arms. "With your head in his mouth."

"That's correct."

Mattie stretched on the windowsill. "It's true, sugar. No one was gonna eat anyone else."

I shook my head. "Well, don't get too friendly. The rabbit isn't staying forever."

"Such vehemence," Collinsworth said. "I wonder what I ever did to warrant your immediate distaste."

I gritted my teeth. "You hide things. You're not upfront until I force you into a corner. My cousin has been arrested for murder. *Murder.* You had information that could've stopped it."

"Maybe. Maybe not," he said in his fake little British accent that made me want to pick him up by his feet and dangle him out the window.

But he was right. Her fingerprints all over the murder weapon? Looked bad. Sounded worse.

Deciding I wouldn't blow my head off my neck in anger on a holiday, I showered and dressed in a pair of brown corduroy pants and a purple turtleneck sweater that Amelia had magicked for me when I was bemoaning that everything I owned was brown.

Actually, it was Cordelia bemoaning the fact. She said my closet looked like the inside of a cave, so Amelia fixed it.

By the time I hopped downstairs with a herd of animals that would've made Dr. Doolittle proud, everyone had arrived.

My aunts Licorice, Licky for short, and Mint were already seated. They were towering redheads and looked nearly identical except Mint had long wavy tresses and Licky had straight silky hair. They even finished each other's sentences. It was pretty annoying, but a corner of my heart belonged just to them.

Garrick Young, sheriff and traitor to the Craple family, had arrived. He stood by the windows, leaning over Cordelia and brushing a long strand of hair from her shoulder.

My chest constricted to the point my next breath came as a gasp. My gaze darted from them and landed on Becky Ray. She wore a shapeless gray dress. Her hair spiraled into frizzy curls around her head, making her look like a deranged angel.

I snagged a glance at Collinsworth, who was hiking up into a chair. Pretentious little guy. I crossed to Becky and placed my hands on her shoulders.

My gut instinct was to ask how she was doing, which was stupid. She was doing terribly. I plastered on a big welcoming smile, gave her a hug and said, "We're so glad to see you. Come in."

Of course running through my head the whole time was, *My cousin didn't kill your sister. Hey, maybe it wasn't such a great idea for me to invite you, and if you'd heard that my cousin is currently in jail for the murder, maybe you shouldn't have come.*

Of course I pursed my lips and kept that inner dialogue tucked quietly away like a secret love letter hidden in my panty drawer.

"Thank you for inviting me," Becky said. She shuffled forward one step, seemed to notice the roomful of redheads and dug her heels in.

"Maybe this wasn't such a good idea."

"Nonsense." I could've kicked myself. "Come in. It'll be fine."

I tucked her into a seat beside me as the rest of the family moved to the dinner table. I peered around and noticed that freaking pecan pie that Betty had dug out of the trash sat on a nice plate on the sideboard.

The thing was half-eaten, with most of the chocolate bat missing.

"Excuse me." I whisked the pie from the table. I made it to the kitchen and had the trash lid lifted before Betty stopped me.

"Hold it right there, kid."

I froze. Freaking busted.

Betty and I locked eyes like we were in a showdown at the OK Corral. "You're not serving this."

Her chin trembled. "I'll do whatever I want."

"This is trash pie."

"It's delicious."

I lowered my voice to a hiss and pointed my finger at her. "Your niece is sitting in jail. This pie could be the reason why. Stop eating it."

Betty reached for it, her hands clutching air. "I want it."

I raised it over my head. Betty was a couple of inches shorter than me, and unless she Inspector Gadgeted her arms to shoot out, I'd be able to keep the pie from her.

"You can't have it. Stop."

"Give it back before I put a boil so big on your butt you won't be able to sit for days."

I narrowed my eyes. "Likely story."

Then I did it. I wished the pie into the top shelf of my closet, all the way in back.

It vanished.

Betty fisted her little hands. "You've got a death wish, kid."

"I love you, too," I chirped, kissing her cheek. "Now let's go have a wonderful Thanksgiving dinner."

Betty puffed behind me as I led us to the dining room. Now that the monstrosity of the pecan pie had been carefully stowed away, dinner could begin.

Which it did—totally awkwardly.

Mint shot a sad puppy-dog look to Becky Ray. "I'm so sorry about your sister."

"Thank you," she sniffed.

"Yes, we were the deepest of friends," Collinsworth said.

Becky Ray fired lasers from her eyes at him. The rabbit shrank into his seat.

Licky, apparently sensing the rising tension, went with the winning, "Terrible about Carmen."

The entire room stopped. Every head turned to Licky and stared at her as if she'd doused her head with gasoline and set it on fire.

Then all gazes swiveled to Becky Ray, who stared at her plate.

Cordelia cut the tension with a spoon. "Lots of giving has been going on in town."

"Oh yes," Licky said. "Mint and I are giving lessons on how to work magic."

"To destroy mankind?" Betty said. She angled her fork at them. "Because that's what y'all do, ruin things."

Mint gasped in mock horror. "We can't help that we're chaos witches. You're the one who bred us; maybe you should be looking at yourself when you point fingers at us."

Licky cleared her throat. Her eyes shone brightly when she pinned her gaze on me. "Heard from Axel?"

The fork and knife slipped from my fingers and clattered to the porcelain plate.

"What?"

Mint frowned like a puppy dog. "That's right. I'd forgotten he left town. I don't know why I'd forgotten, but y'all were dating. Why'd he go?"

I shook my head. "I don't think this is good Thanksgiving dinner talk."

Licky reached out and squeezed my arm. "But we're here for you. We want to know your problems. Your problems are our problems."

"How else are you going to heal if you don't talk about it and purge it from your system?" Mint said.

I stared at my plate of chicken poulet. I felt my brows pinch together so tightly if a zit had been in the fold of skin it would've burst. "Mmm. Yeah. He just couldn't deal with being a werewolf in this town. Too many problems had occurred because of it. He didn't want anyone to get hurt."

"Or he didn't want you to get hurt?" Mint said.

"Yeah. That."

"I think it was brave of him to leave," Licky said.

"Sounds like a scaredy cat, if you ask me." Becky Ray had finally spoken.

We stared at her.

She shrugged. "Problems aren't meant to be run from. They're meant to be faced head-on."

The words were a punch to the gut. Problems. I'd been running from problems too before Axel left. I'd lived in tortuous fear that he would discover I cared about him, things would get heated and then he'd run screaming for the hills.

Turned out he ran for the hills, but for a completely different reason. Because the fact that he'd nearly attacked and killed me had wounded him in a way I would never understand.

That was the honest-to-goodness shocking truth. I didn't have to live in fear that I would accidentally kill Axel. But one night a month that thought consumed him. When the reality almost occurred, it must've broken him.

I shook my head. It took everything I had not to drop my face in my palms.

It could've broken him. I don't know. He. Never. Called.

And honestly I never talked about it with my family because the wound was so raw. Axel's leaving had scraped my insides completely clean. I was a shell that didn't know what to think or feel.

I loved Axel, but this was too much. Leaving me when we were just getting started, when our love had begun to burn bright was a stain on my heart that I couldn't erase. I don't even know if Wite-Out would work.

Betty shifted the conversation like a pro. "Licky, Mint, tell us how these magic lessons you're giving won't cause trouble."

Lickey threaded her hands while smiling with delight. "Mama, I am so glad you asked. Take this turkey here."

We all stared at the glistening golden bird. One breast had been carved completely away, leaving the breastbone jutting out.

Becky glanced at it skeptically. "What about it?"

Mint leaned forward. "We could make it more juicy. Better tasting."

"How?" Amelia said. "It's already so juicy. Betty's outdone herself."

"I agree," Betty said.

Licky rolled her eyes. "What if it wasn't so good?"

"Say it needed help," Mint added.

"That's where we come in," Licky said.

"We teach how to make it better flavored," Mint said, snapping her fingers. "Like that."

A gust of magic swooshed down the table and coiled around the carcass. I held my breath, waiting to see what would happen.

Probably nothing.

"I'll try a bite." Garrick stretched his hand and grabbed the leg. The turkey bolted straight up, out of his grasp. The leg bones rotated down until the thing appeared to be standing on stilts. It jumped from the dish and onto the table.

Collinsworth screamed. Becky Ray screamed.

After that, the entire table turned into bouts of screams that sounded like blasts from a shotgun. I fell back in my chair, knocking my head against the floor.

Air escaped from my lungs in a *humph*.

The turkey catapulted to the rug and ran a circle around the living room. With a skeletal wing, the thing grabbed the door handle, opened it, and raced out the porch and down the block.

I brushed myself off and managed to get to my feet on quaking legs.

Betty pointed a finger at Mint and Licky. "Get my Thanksgiving dinner back. I wasn't through eating it."

NINE

*N*eedless to say, once the turkey was tracked down and returned to its place on the dining table, my appetite had vanished.

There was something grosser than gross about munching on a carcass that had been running only seconds before.

Nope, that wasn't quite right.

There was something *absolutely disgusting* about the idea of a dead bird galloping about, flapping naked, cooked wings like it was trying to take flight.

Yep. That was more appropriate.

Once dinner was finished, everyone left except for Garrick, who hung around sipping coffee and chatting with the new and improved —meaning nice—Cordelia.

Seriously, it was very strange.

Matter of fact, folks were still having Free Stuff Sales on their lawns.

I stepped onto the porch and watched our neighbors cataloging their giveaways when a puff of smoke took me by surprise.

Becky Ray sat on the porch swing vaping something that smelled mildly of black pepper.

"I am sorry about Lori Lou," I said.

She took another drag. "Thank you. It was always Lori's dream to own a shop."

I nibbled my bottom lip. I had no idea if Becky knew the information Collinsworth had told me. Time to find out.

"Did you know Lori Lou was selling love potions illegally?"

Becky Ray choked. I muscled the porch swing to a stop and whacked her back a few times.

"No," she said. "What are you talking about?"

I sighed. "Something I heard."

Her eyes narrowed to slitty wedges of death. "Who said it? The rabbit? What a joke." She sneered and turned away, shaking her head in disgust.

"I can't say who I heard it from."

"It was Collinsworth. That little fibber. Let me tell you something about that rabbit."

"I wish you would."

Becky Ray eyed the front door like she wanted to stomp in there and punch the bunny in the face. I do not condone animal cruelty. Not at all, but honest-to-Jesus truth, that was the look she had.

"If anyone talked Lori Lou into it, it would've been Collinsworth."

"What?"

She killed the vapor streaming from the stick. "Yep. That little guy. He had Lori Lou wrapped around his finger. I mean, who ever heard of a rabbit working in a bakery?"

"I hadn't."

"And no one else in their right mind would believe it, either. But those two were so close. I never trusted that bunny. Like I said, if she was doing that, it was probably his idea."

"What about the trash bags outside the shop? Some were left last night and were gone this morning."

She looked away, bored. "I don't know anything about them." Becky Ray rose and stretched her arms over her head, revealing a muffin top that I'll never be able to unsee in my entire life.

Thanks, Becky Ray.

I leaned my arm against a column. "Do you think it's weird that people are giving things away?"

She grunted. "Why would I? It's Thanksgiving."

Why did everyone keep saying that? "It's about giving thanks, not giving things away."

Becky shrugged noncommittally.

"You staying for a while?"

"Maybe a few more days. I need to get my head on straight. Make sure they've got the right killer." Her gaze flickered back to the house.

"You won't be taking Collinsworth with you?"

She laughed. It sounded like a woman who'd chain-smoked giant life-size cigars her entire life. "No. We hate each other."

As she walked away, I mumbled, "So he's said."

Betty cornered me as soon as I entered the house. Her eyes were inky black, the irises huge. She clawed at me. "Where's the pie?"

I braced my hands in front of me. "You're not getting it. It's gone."

"No." She ran into the kitchen, I presume to make more pie. Apparently it was an incredibly addictive confection. Maybe I should've tried some.

"Sheesh. What is in that pie?"

Cordelia glanced over her shoulder at me and said teasingly, "It was good."

"So good it made you nice."

"Sure did," Amelia said. She winked at me. "But it didn't make me anything. I'm the same. But anyway, I wonder if when we light the town Christmas tree tonight, if it'll be really bright?"

Something flashed in Cordelia's eyes. I knew it was a retort of brilliance. Something so cataclysmically dark and scathing that it was on the tip of her tongue. The old Cordelia wouldn't for a second have stopped herself from ripping a sword of words through Amelia's stomach. But this new Cordelia...

"I'm sure it'll be bright," she said in a sickening bubble-gum voice.

Amelia shot me a concerned look. I smirked. "Looks like the whole nice thing is hanging around."

Garrick wove his fingers through hers. "She's always been nice to me."

"Consider yourself lucky," Amelia said.

Deciding it was time to break up that conversation, I steered Amelia toward the stairs. "Don't you think something weird is going on?"

She tugged her blonde pixie cut. "Like what?"

"Everyone's giving things away. It's so all of a sudden. And Betty and that pie—sheesh. She pulled it out of the trash."

"I heard that," my grandmother shouted from the kitchen.

"Do you have a horn butted up to your ear?" I said.

"Yes," she said.

I stared at the ceiling and counted to ten. How annoying.

"What are you saying?" Amelia said.

"I don't know." I dropped my voice farther. "But Collinsworth said that Lori Lou was selling love potions illegally."

Amelia clasped her hands over her mouth. "Love potions!" she practically shouted. Great. Now Garrick knew exactly what we were talking about.

I pulled her up the stairs, into my room and shut the door. Though now we had an audience that resembled more of a barnyard than anything else, it was still out of earshot of my family.

"Yes." I glanced at Collinsworth. "I'm telling her about the love potions."

"The ones I might be killed for," he said.

I rolled my eyes. "Yes. Okay. You're protected while you're here. No one's going to harm you." I turned back to Amelia. "I think the town is acting weird. Something is up. Rabbit, do you know anything about it?"

He hopped on the bed and let his short feet dangle off the side. "Nothing. I don't know anything."

Lying again. I could feel it. I couldn't force him to reveal anything he didn't want. But my suspicion that he was hiding information was like a pin poking my side.

Amelia rubbed my arm. "I'm sure everything will be fine. You'll see. You're coming to the Christmas tree lighting tonight?"

"First I'm hearing of it."

She clapped with glee. "On Thanksgiving night the town all convenes on Bubbling Cauldron to witness the lighting of the town tree. It's so much fun. It's magical. You have to attend."

I scratched my head. "Okay. Sure. I'll be there."

For the second time in the past couple of days I wished Axel were here. He would've believed me, would've smelled the same weirdness I did.

I sighed. All heads turned to me. "It's nothing."

My phone buzzed from its place on my pillow. I picked it up and didn't recognize the number. It was out of town, but not too far away.

My heart thundered to an explosive stop. "It's Axel."

Amelia opened her lids so wide I thought her eyes might splat to the floor. "Do you want me to leave?"

I palmed the phone. "Yes. Mattie, can you take the animals with you, too?"

Mattie jumped from the windowsill and trotted to the door. "Come on, y'all, Pepper needs private time."

They nearly tripped over each other to clamber from the room. Meanwhile, I counted the rings because there's only six before the call hits voice mail.

"Four," I whispered.

"Five."

They were gone. I kicked the door at the same time as I swiped a finger across the bottom bar. "Hello?"

Nothing. If this was a stupid telemarketing call on Thanksgiving, I would get someone fired.

"Hello?" I repeated.

"Pepper." The low male voice crackled into my ear.

The reception wasn't great. I crossed to the window and nearly stuck my head through the pane of glass. "Yes?"

"Happy Thanksgiving."

A slow, creeping realization sank into my brain like icing melting on a warm cake.

"Oh my God. Rufus?" I couldn't believe it.

"Yes. Not expecting me?"

"No." I paused. "Why're you calling me? How did you get my number? Are you stalking me?"

"It's a listed number. I only wanted to wish you a happy Thanksgiving."

I could hang up, forget he ever rang, but there was a pie sitting on the top shelf of my closet along with a suspicion that crap wasn't right in Magnolia Cove, y'all.

I clutched the phone to my jaw. "I'm so glad you called. I need your help."

TEN

"*I* don't even get a happy Thanksgiving first? I'm hurt."

I seethed into the phone. "Happy Thanksgiving. You're lucky I don't call the police and have them trace this call."

Rufus paused. "I thought you needed my help."

I stopped. "I do." I sighed. "There's something strange going on here."

"In Magnolia Cove? The most magical place on earth?" His voice dripped with sarcasm. It irritated the holy heck out of me.

"Impossible," he said.

"It's not. Seriously, Rufus." His name set my tongue on fire. What's wrong with me?

I was obviously severely screwed up in knots over Axel. Had to be. So much so that when Rufus called, I didn't know my head from my butt crack.

"Okay." He relented. "What's wrong?"

"There was a woman here. Here name was Lori Lou Fick. She opened up a bakery across the street from Carmen's. To make a long, boring story—"

"Nothing you say is ever boring."

"I could kill you right now. Can you please just listen? What's wrong with you? We're mortal enemies."

"I forgot." A touch of something rang in his voice. Was it sadness? Weird.

"Lori handed out pecan pies with little chocolate bats in them. Now everyone's giving their things away."

"It is Thanksgiving."

"That's not what Thanksgiving's about!"

Rufus replied with a buttery laugh. "Point taken. You think the pies have something to do with it?"

"Lori's dead. Murdered with a pair of ribbon-cutting scissors. Her pet rabbit told me that she was selling love potions illegally. I saw a car filled with men screech from the back of her building this morning. I have their license plate."

"Has Axel run it?"

My stomach exploded into the earth. He didn't know. Rufus had no clue that Axel had left.

I tapped a clenched fist to my forehead. "No. Axel doesn't know. He's gone."

"Gone? Why would the wolf leave?"

There was a test in his voice. A test and I didn't know if I would fail or score sun-blistering high marks.

"Never mind," was all I managed to say. I couldn't go into it. Didn't want to go into it. "But no. Axel hasn't run it."

"Are you asking me to?"

I gnashed my teeth. I wished I had a piece of beef jerky to tear off and chew to a knobby pulp. But I didn't. All I had was my tongue, and I wasn't about to gnaw that raw.

I closed my eyes and sighed. "Yes. I'm asking if you'll run the plate."

"Do you have any pie left?"

"Yes."

"I can analyze it. See what's in it."

"In your Frankenstein lab?"

He laughed faintly. "No. I do know how to work magic to analyze things. Just like your boyfriend." I couldn't help but note a touch of bitterness in his voice at the word *boyfriend*.

This was the break I'd been waiting for. No one would help me on this. Everyone thought I was crazy, and the one creature who knew the truth—stupid Collinsworth—was holding on to his secrets tighter than a high schooler locking down her virginity the night before prom.

I huffed out a breath. "When and where?"

"When do you want to meet?"

It sounded like a challenge. I didn't know if it was, and to be honest, I wasn't up for any sort of challenge. This wasn't a game. These were real people I knew being affected by something that was beyond my level of understanding.

"I can meet tonight."

I swore it sounded like he smiled. "Are you going to the Christmas tree lighting?"

I frowned. "How do you know about that?"

"I used to live there, remember?" he said, sounding annoyed.

"Right. Yes, I'm going."

"Meet me right after the bulbs are lit. You won't be missed that way."

"Where?"

"Do you remember, once upon a time when I wanted your power?" Regret dripped from the words.

"I do. But I don't think that's over. I believe you still want my magic."

"I'll settle for friendship."

"And weird calls on holidays?"

He chuckled. "Yes, and those. But do you remember when you tried to leave town and I found you on the outskirts? You were on the road."

My stomach clenched. I remembered. If it hadn't been for Axel, Rufus would've captured me. Then he would've analyzed my brain, made me become his cohort in evil. Or whatever it was he wanted.

I gulped. The memory was too real, too sharp. "I remember."

"Meet me there. Bring the pie."

Click.

"And goodbye to you, too," I said. I glanced at the closet. "Now how the heck am I going to smuggle this out without Betty knowing?"

That woman was like a feral dog around the pie. I had to think of something.

It hit me like a bright, brilliant shooting star slamming into my chest.

I snapped my fingers. "I've got it."

"WHAT'S IN YOUR PURSE?" Betty sniffed the opening of my bag.

We were on our way to the tree lighting. I knew she would be all over me, trying to find that stupid pie.

"Just regular stuff. Lipstick, tissues, tampons."

Betty glared. "Where's my pie?"

I shook my head. "I have no idea what you're talking about."

She wagged a fist. I bit back the laugh that threatened to blow from my mouth. "I'll find my pie."

I squeezed her shoulders. "Why don't we enjoy the tree lighting and forget about the pie?"

Though most of the homes in town still had furniture strewn on the lawns, a couple of them showcased something that made my gut twist.

"For Giving?" I murmured.

The sign staked in the yard of a cute white cottage stole my breath. "For Giving?" I repeated.

Betty harrumphed. "That's Sylvia Spirits's house."

The black letters of the sign confused me. "What does that even mean?"

Amelia popped up between us. "I don't know."

"Excuse me," came a voice at my ankle. Collinsworth tugged my pant leg.

"What is it?" *Be grateful I don't kick you.*

"I believe," the rabbit enunciated perfectly, "the sign signifies that the owner is giving away the house."

I screeched to a halt. "No way. Why would Sylvia be giving away her house?"

Collinsworth snapped his little trap shut.

I nudged him with my toe. "Why would she be giving her house away?"

"She's in the spirit of giving," Betty said.

"Makes no sense," I ground out. "None of this makes any sense."

I raked my fingers through my hair. This whole situation was like a horrible virus. With every mutation the scenario worsened. At first it was folks handing out small things. Now we were talking houses.

I needed to speak with Rufus.

A shudder swept through my body. Never in the entire history of the world did I think I'd need to speak with Rufus. Comets would destroy the planet first. A meteor would smack me right in the chest before I sought Rufus's help.

I scanned the sky for said comet but saw nothing. It wouldn't have surprised me if the stupid thing collided with my backside.

After what seemed like a constant battle to keep my purse away from a snooping Betty, we finally reached the tree.

My breath staggered.

It was magnificent. It must've stood at least twenty feet tall. Endless strands of bulbs on rope twisted all the way to the top. Nestled in the boughs were decorations completely individualized to Magnolia Cove.

There were witches in Christmas clothes, giants playing in the snow, and cats sitting atop red and green pumpkins. The ornaments were absolutely darling. I loved them all.

My heart was near to bursting at the magic of the holidays in Magnolia Cove.

Too bad someone had to be murdered and now everyone was acting all goofy.

Oh, and let's not forget that I was actually looking forward to meeting up with Rufus so he could help me untangle this mess.

Yes. That's when I knew I must've been suffering from some sort of brain damage. When the thought of Rufus Mayes made me want to run as quickly as I could to meet him, I knew I was either suffering from the same virus as everyone else, or I was infected with my own original virus.

I was pretty sure there wasn't a cure other than hiding under a rock and never seeing the light of day again.

I guess what I meant was—I hoped we got this whole mess figured out because the thought of relying on Rufus made my stomach do something I wasn't familiar with.

I decided not to think about it too much.

My thoughts flashed to Axel, but that was even worse, so I concentrated on counting how many witch ornaments decorated my side of the tree.

"Hi, Amelia."

All of us twisted our heads to the left.

Sidling up to the group, apparently on soundless loafers, was Dicky Downy. He brushed 1960's surfer boy bangs from his eyes.

Amelia gazed at him with mistrust. "Hi, Dicky."

He punched his hands into his pockets and stared at the ground. I swear if there'd been a pebble to kick, he would've done it. "Happy Thanksgiving."

She sniffed. "Same to you."

All of us, including myself, were totally glued to this exchange. What was the big mystery here? Dicky was clearly smitten with Amelia, and my pixie-haircut, doe-eyed, almost airheaded cousin looked at Dicky Downy with confusion.

Since Dicky was here and he'd had a tiff with Lori Lou the day before she was murdered, I decided his brain was ripe for plucking.

"How was the pie from the Sweet Witch?"

"Good," he mumbled, still staring at Amelia.

"Terrible about Lori Lou."

He raked his fingers through his hair. "I'd say." He reached out as if he wanted to graze his fingers down Amelia's arm and stopped himself when her gaze snapped to his hand. "I'm giving tours of my parents' house. Would you like to come?"

"A tour before the Christmas tours start?" Betty huffed.

"It's my way of giving back to the community."

Amelia gave him a murderous look. "And what else will you be giving away?"

"Nothing."

Right. Dicky had been the rich kid who sold the drugs. I turned to face him, placing myself between him and Amelia. Now he had no choice but to look at me.

"Dicky." I tapped my finger to my cheek. "I heard the strangest rumor about you. About way back in the day when you were in school here."

"What's that?"

I lowered my voice. "That you were always well supplied with...things."

His expression remained blank for what felt like an entire minute. Finally recognition flared in his eyes. "Right. That."

I was about to make myself look horrible, but I had to get Carmen out of jail. I had to prove that Lori Lou was killed because of this whole illegal-love-potion thing. I just had to.

"There's something I wanted to experiment with." I dropped my voice even lower. "Love potion?"

Dicky rocked back. "Yeah. I don't do any of that anymore."

I searched his eyes for a hint of a lie. The blue irises didn't flicker with anything other than absolute honesty. So Dicky wasn't buying love potions. But who was?

I wish that little jerk Collinsworth would just tell me. I gazed down at him. The rabbit wore the handkerchief he'd nabbed from the bakery. White poppies floated over the crimson as if they were drowning in paint.

"Thanks anyway," I said, turning back.

Dicky moved closer to Amelia, and I stepped back, waiting for the tree to be lit.

Mayor Battle stepped onto a podium. He cupped a hand under his mouth. Magic unfurled from his palm. When he spoke, his voice bellowed in high definition.

"Happy Thanksgiving! Welcome. I won't give a big speech. We're all here to see one thing. This tree lit up. Without further ado, light her!"

The bulbs hummed and flickered for a second before blazing to life. I swear, if Santa Claus was cruising around scoping out his route for the big day, he would've seen this tree's lights from China.

Yes, they were that bright.

Which meant it was time for me to meet my nemesis—Rufus Mayes.

ELEVEN

$\mathcal{I}$ sneaked back to the house and snatched my cast-iron riding skillet from its spot by the hearth. Once outside I hiked one leg over and jetted into the sky.

Lifting off, soaring across the horizon as the stars winked to life was something I would never get used to. The bottom dropped away from my stomach as the tip of the skillet sliced through the atmosphere.

I landed on the road outside town a few minutes later. The canopy of trees overhead made the growing dark almost menacing. I pulled a flashlight from my pocket and washed it over the trees.

A figure stepped from the shadows. I shot my beam over. He wore black jeans and a soft black sweater. His long, dark hair had been cut to his shoulders, and the black eyeliner that normally rimmed his eyes was gone.

I did a double take. "Rufus?"

He sauntered over. "The one and only." He opened his arms. "What? No hug?"

I stiffened. "I'd rather hug Satan." Which wasn't true, but Rufus wasn't my favorite person on the planet, either.

He traced his thumb over his bottom lip. "Understood. Now. You have something for me?"

My stomach plunged. Odd. Was it the fact that he was getting right to business? We'd sort of called a truce last time I met him. A flash of something burned bright in my core. Sadness? Was I sad that he wasn't talking to me?

Ridiculous.

But just to test it...

"How've you been?" I said.

"Almost sounds like you care."

"You wish." I glanced away.

"I've been remarkably good for someone condemned from all decent society."

"Glad to know something's working out for you." Really, I was. "What about the experiments? Been playing vampire on any unsuspecting victims? Or trying to turn them into vampires? Or whatever it is you do."

He took a step forward. My heart leaped to my throat. I'd never noticed before how dark his eyes were—inky black. They were so dark I couldn't tell where the pupil stopped and the iris began. I was tempted to flash my light in them just to see.

His lip coiled into a smirk. "It seems I've taken over a new leaf."

"Shocking."

He chuckled. "I haven't done any of those things since I left here. I've actually been a model citizen."

"Hard to believe."

He laughed softly. "I knew you'd say that. There's no way for me to prove it to you."

"And there's no way this town is going to allow you in to confirm it."

"I know." His voice became dark, bothered. He inhaled sharply. Rufus's gaze flickered to my throat. "Your heart's beating fast."

I slapped my neck. "I don't know what you're talking about. Look, it's been a weird couple of days."

"Tell me about it."

It sounded like there was a deeper subtext. *Like, tell me all your pain. Vomit on me like I'm a toilet.*

"Um. Like I said, a woman was murdered. It was rumored she'd been selling love potions. I've got the tag number of a vehicle and a sample of a pie. I need to know what's in it. Everyone's acting weird."

He arched an eyebrow. "And that's different from how they all normally act, why?"

I rolled my eyes. "It just is. Look, can you help?"

He took another step forward. Heat wafted off his body. I glanced at his shoulders and noticed lines of muscle I'd never seen before. Why would I have? I'd never paid attention.

His eyes smiled at me. I shivered. "There's nothing more I'd like than to help you, Pepper Dunn."

I leaned back and lost my balance. Without missing a beat, Rufus hooked an arm around my waist and yanked me forward. My palms pressed his chest. I was touching him. I was touching my archnemesis. The heat radiating from him felt like a thousand light bulbs beneath my fingers.

I yanked back, giving myself at least three feet of space between our bodies.

"I need the pie."

Right. The pie. I grimaced. "Give me a minute."

There had seriously been no other place to stick it than my pants. Betty had been sniffing around me like a dog in heat for the stupid bit of pecans and chocolate. There hadn't been another option.

I showed him my back while I yanked the Saran wrapped confection from its spot. I fanned it, trying to get my body heat off. I did not feel comfortable handing Rufus Mayes something that had basically kissed my crotch.

After a couple of seconds I turned around. "Here it is."

"I'm not going to ask where you hid it."

"Thank you."

"Because I already know."

I nearly growled at him. "Do you want it or not?"

He flattened his palm to his chest. "Because I'm a gentleman, I'll ask you to unwrap it and place it on the ground."

"You're going to do it here?" The shock in my voice was obvious.

"Of course. I'm going to give you whatever answers I can. Now."

I peeled back the clear covering to reveal the smooshed and deformed pie. It looked like roadkill. Luckily it smelled a thousand times better.

Rufus knelt over it. He tipped his head one way and then the other. Moonlight splashed against his jaw, showcasing the straight line. When his gaze met mine, I felt like I'd been busted.

"You have to tell me one thing first."

"What?" My throat was so dry.

"What happened to Axel?"

"Anything else."

He rose. "No deal then."

"A friend wouldn't make me tell you something I didn't want to."

He smiled, amused. "Maybe I can help."

"I doubt it."

"You doubt too much."

My stomach quaked. A million butterflies flapped their wings into a tornado. I pressed the heels of my hands to my eyes. Maybe I would feel better after I said it.

"He left because he almost killed me the night he got loose. The night when it was endless Halloween."

Rufus nodded. He stared at the ground. It was impossible to read his expression. And I wanted to. I really, really wanted to.

How flipping annoying.

"He doesn't want to hurt you," Rufus finally said. "You mean too much to him. It's the curse of the werewolf. Almost impossible to maintain a real relationship with someone."

"I guess."

"I'm sorry." When his gaze locked on mine, the expression on his face told me it was true.

"It's not your fault."

He nodded.

"Do you think he'll come back?"

What was I saying? Why was I asking Rufus to analyze my relationship with Axel.

"Do you want him to?" he said carefully.

"Yes." Without a doubt. My heart ached for Axel. His absence made me realize exactly how shattered I was over his leaving. I'd bottled so much of my feelings that the truth burst through the dam I'd created around my cracked heart.

He raised a hand over the pie. "Let's see what we have in here." Rufus concentrated. A stream of magic flowed into the pie. "You can help."

"How?"

Rufus's brow was pinched so tight he almost looked handsome. Handsome? I must've been coming down with a horrible virus.

"Hold my hand and you'll find out."

I gulped. "Is this some trick? If I touch you, you're going to steal me from here, aren't you? You'll chain me to a warped dungeon full of beakers filled with disgusting black liquid that smells rank."

"You do think a lot of yourself, don't you?" But he said it with a wry smile.

"Only reacting to what you've taught me."

"Here. I'll teach you to use your powers more. Touch my hand. Right on top. I won't reach for you. I won't press you. This is only for your benefit."

I teetered. "How much pressure do I have to use?"

A glimmer of something brightened in his eyes. "As little as you like. If you only want to touch me with the pad of your very delicate pinky, you may."

"I'm not delicate."

"You're not? Could've fooled me." He spread his fingers. "I'm about to start. If you're game, play. If you're not, stand back. The power will be, shall we say, a bit intense."

Not one to be called a coward, I smacked my palm onto his hand. Delicate pinky, my foot. He'd get as much skin as my fearful mind could bear.

The smirk that lined his face told me my challenge amused him. "And here we go. The spell I'm using is one to draw out the crux of the magic in the pie." He watched the pecan goo as if he were afraid it would jump up and run away.

That was always a possibility. Thanksgiving dinner proved that.

He nodded to me. "With your head witch abilities this would be an easy spell for you."

"If I knew what I was doing."

"That's why I'm teaching you. You'll never reach your full potential —oh wait, that's too scary of a thought for you. You'll never reach *any* potential unless you stretch yourself."

I bit back the urge to tell Rufus he didn't know what he was talking about. But the truth was that he did know. He knew my fears and understood the dark anxiety that plagued me about my ability.

Jerk.

"Watch and learn."

Magic poured from his hand. His skin burned bright. The light seeped into me. I thought my hand would catch fire, but there wasn't any heat. It was pure light.

It was glorious.

The pie peeled apart, unfolding to a mess of syrup. The last remnants of the chocolate bat melted, mingling with the crust and filling. It broke apart and glued together, eventually forming another shape. One that was completely different.

"A heart," I whispered.

Did this mean the pie had been spelled to be a love potion? That didn't make any sense. No one was falling in love; they were simply donating their life's treasures to one another.

The light in Rufus faded. I blinked away the bright dots mangling my vision.

"What was that?"

He rose. Rufus stretched to full height. I'd never known how tall he was before. Never noticed the line of his shoulders or how soft his T-shirt looked on him.

Of course, Rufus normally wore whips and chains, so seeing him in a normal material nearly made my head pop off my neck.

He took my hand. A tiny gasp wheezed from my lips. His flesh still contained the memory of the spell. It tattooed itself into my brain. The raw power hummed in my bones.

He studied me. "What do you think it was? That spell."

I quirked a brow. "I thought you'd tell me."

"You thought wrong. You're smart enough to figure it out."

I paused and let my mind settle. The dust flitted away. "It was a truth spell."

"Go on." He smiled.

I peered into the forest. "You wanted the truth." My gaze flickered to him. "That's where the light came from."

The corner of his lip coiled into what some other woman might think was a delicious smile. "The light of truth. It's very cliché, don't you think?"

"It's not like you and I are superheroes."

"Speak for yourself."

He dropped my hand and pointed to the pile of pie. "I wanted the truth, so that's what I focused on. There is some magic a wizard can do where the honesty of the spell takes the lead and gives you knowledge. This is one of those spells."

I stepped back. "Are you saying the purity of your heart is what makes the magic work?"

He smirked. "You'd love that, wouldn't you? Me saying I'm pure."

"I don't know what you're talking about." Would he quit the playful banter and get on with it?

"The spell worked. The shape."

"The heart?" I glanced around him.

"The heart is a basic magical shape—so are circles, triangles, stars —things that are normal to you and I. But the heart is special. It means something specific."

"The pie has a magic spell on it."

He cocked his head back and grinned. "Ah, it means more than that. If it were that simple, the spell would've been uncovered and realized for what it was ages ago. No, this is complex magic."

I frowned. "I don't understand."

"It's a spell hidden within a spell. That's what the heart means. The first layer of the spell ensures the target doesn't realize that they're under control by magic."

My heart pounded. "And the second layer?"

Rufus's eyes darkened. Was he angry? Ticked? Jealous that he hadn't worked the spell first? Probably that was it.

"The second part," he said sharply, "creates something very nasty in whoever comes under the influence."

"What?"

He pinched his lips shut for a moment. Rufus exhaled. "The second part of the spell creates an addict."

"You mean the person would be addicted to the pie?" Impossible. Ridiculous. But still…all signs pointed to yes.

Rufus leaned over until we were eye level. He squeezed my shoulder, sending a jolt of electricity to my toes. "The sad person who eats this dessert and doesn't get any more of it will go into violent withdrawals."

"How violent?"

Rufus's jaw clenched. "So violent they could die."

TWELVE

I flew back to the house in record time. I landed on the grass hard, nearly tipping over. Yet somehow I managed to plant my heels and stop my forward descent.

Call it good old-fashioned Southern gal temper that did it. I was so full of spit, fire and sass I could've karate chopped a tree down.

I barreled inside, stowed my skillet by the fire and assessed the situation.

"Hey," I said to Cordelia and Betty.

They both sat lazed in the living room. Betty was reading *The Witch's Almanac*, a publication that probably told her the best time to sprout zits on our butts—you know when they would last the longest, hurt the most, that sort of thing.

Of course, she'd only do it if she was angry at us. Or about to die from withdrawals.

Cordelia dragged her gaze from her phone to me. My cousin was all glassy-eyed like she was one step away from a high fever.

Betty had the same look on her face.

Great. I had work to do.

They both gave me a lazy "hey." I bolted up the stairs and crashed into my room.

The animals stared at me as if I had three heads. Yep, because two obviously wasn't enough.

I whirled around until I spotted Collinsworth sitting on a chair with a cup of tea in his paws.

"Rabbit," I seethed. "Tell me everything."

"I've told you all I know."

Stupid fake British accent.

I cemented my hands on the arms of the chair, pinning him. "No. You haven't."

Mattie stretched and yawned in her lazy cat way. "What're you talkin' 'bout, sugar bear?"

I glowered. "The pie that Betty dug up from the trash is spelled to create addicts. People who have to continue eating it. It's obviously dosed with some sort of giving potion as well since everyone's handing their stuff away."

I bent down so far I was nearly touching the rabbit's twitching nose. "At first I thought the giving spell was the worst part of it, but now I realize it's not. The worst part is that we're going to have a few hundred people suffering from withdrawals so bad they could die. What's the cure, rabbit?"

"I-I-I don't know."

"I don't believe you." I pointed at my door. "There are two people downstairs who won't be getting any more pie because Lori Lou is gone and the bakery is shut down. Unless Becky Ray decides to reopen, but she's not doing that."

I poked his chest. "She doesn't like you, remember? You had to sneak around at night to get your favorite handkerchief of Lori Lou's. You wouldn't have done that if you trusted Becky."

I stared at him. The rabbit quivered and shook. The teacup rattled on its saucer. "Rabbit. I need your help."

He didn't budge. From my back pocket made entirely of air, I yanked the only card I had left. "If you don't help me, I'll be going to Becky Ray for help."

I turned and headed toward the door.

"No! Wait!"

I smiled victoriously.

I clapped my hands and turned, throwing him a stare made of dragon fire. "What?" I snapped.

"I'll help," he squeaked.

"How?"

He took a sip of tea before settling the cup and saucer on a table. "I may know of a way to counter the spell."

"Why was there a spell to begin with? What the heck, rabbit? I've been nothing but nice to your sorry cottontail, and all I get in return are lies on top of more lies."

"It's not a lie. Only omissions."

"Yeah, that makes a difference." I huffed and slumped onto the bed. I dropped my face into my hands and tamped down the tidal wave of emotion threatening to clamber up my throat and choke me to death.

It was beginning to be too much. Touching Rufus, missing Axel, stupid pecan pie, Carmen in jail, the cooked turkey running around as if it were alive.

It was enough to make me crack. I felt the split. It started in my head, just above my right eyebrow. I could feel my sense of control loosening, being strangled by the craziness that had overtaken Magnolia Cove.

The worst thought popped into my head. *It would've been bearable if Axel had been here.*

Well, time to toughen up, sweet cakes, 'cause Axel was a no-show. He hadn't even called on the holiday. You know who did call?

Rufus. The man I hate.

A breath staggered from me. A tiny paw touched my knee. I raked my fingers down my face and then up and through my hair before tilting to look.

Collinsworth blinked at me. "We must get into the bakery."

I clenched my fists. "No more lies."

He paused.

"No more," I nearly shouted.

"No more," he repeated quietly.

"Any question I ask, you tell the truth."

He nodded.

I glared so hard I wanted him to break. But to the rabbit's benefit, he stared vacantly back. I shouldered my purse and filled my chest with air until it was puffed up.

"Come on, Mattie. It's time to save Thanksgiving."

She yawned. "And I was hoping we'd be saving Christmas."

I scoffed. "Don't count that out yet."

I CONSIDERED DRAGGING Amelia with us but knew she'd eaten some of Lori Lou's goods. So had Carmen. Amelia wasn't acting strange like my grandmother and Cordelia, bless their hearts, but the idea of bringing her made me uneasy.

When we reached the back door of the Sweet Witch, I grabbed the saw that was still hidden behind some crates and broke the lock that had been replaced. Probably by Becky Ray.

When we got inside, Collinsworth hopped immediately to the kitchen.

"Talk." I dropped my purse on a counter and started flipping lights. "Tell me why Lori Lou spelled the pies."

He pointed to a large mixing bowl. I took it from the shelf and laid it on the counter.

"The giving spell was a mistake," he explained. "Lori Lou was testing out a new recipe and it ended up in the pies."

"All the pies?"

"No. Only some of them." He pawed open a tub. "Here's the flour."

I slid it over to the bowl. "Why would she do that? Test a recipe?"

"Well, um…" He stopped.

Mattie landed on the counter a few feet away. "Rabbit, you better start talkin' or I'm gonna be thinkin' of you as my next tasty treat."

Way to threaten, Mattie. For some reason I felt horrible threatening to cook the rabbit—sort of an animal rights thing, I guess. But when the cat talked about turning him into bunny fricassee, somehow the whole situation felt a lot better.

Sort of bittersweet, I guess you could say.

While Collinsworth told me about Lori Lou, he directed me on how much of each ingredient to add to the bowl.

"It was all my fault." Collinsworth broke into fake British-accented tears. "I'm the one who suggested it. See, when I first met Lori Lou, I was a lowly show rabbit. A magician's pet, waiting for my next go at being pulled from a hat. The magician and Lori dated. That's how I discovered she could bake. There was something special about Lori's confections. Eventually we realized our love for each other. She took me away from the magician, and we began our life together."

"This sounds seriously screwed up." It popped from my mouth before I could sensor it.

"It was platonic, the love of companionship. The magician had connections in the world. Dark connections. Lori Lou dabbled with spells. She made the best love potions I'd ever known. They never lasted long, but that's when I first got the idea. Make a few extra bucks and help people."

"Interesting." Under his direction I dumped sugar into the bowl.

"She was broke. Working as an assistant to an evil woman who never gave Lori Lou credit for her work. With my help she began perfecting her love potion. Then I found a buyer. The money started rolling in, but Lori wanted a store. A shop of her own."

"That's where Becky Ray came in."

"Exactly. Becky Ray could bake as well, and let's face it, her personality is a bit rough."

"Agreed. So she baked while Lori Lou was the face of the business."

"Right again. They'd had another baker, but that didn't go well." He eyed the mixture. "You need to mix your wet ingredients separately."

"Thanks. Why didn't it go well?"

He paused. "It just didn't."

"Rabbit," I warned. "Mattie looks hungry."

"Okay, it didn't go well because the same thing happened."

My jaw dropped. "The entire town ended up spelled?"

"Yes. It was horrible. I told Lori Lou to just stick to selling her potions under the table, but she made a mistake. She had a way about that. She was a little, I don't know how to put it, a little dense or slow in those things. She wanted to help people, she really did, but in her desire to help, things went bad. Just like now."

"Hmm. And what about Becky Ray?"

He sniffed. "What about her?"

"She knows all this, right?"

"Of course she does. She was in on it."

But that's not how Becky had acted. In fact Becky had made it seem that she didn't know anything about her sister's doings.

"What happened in the other town? In regard to Becky." I was pushing. Would he give?

The rabbit nudged a bottle of vanilla toward me. "She was furious. Becky Ray said that all the hard work of opening a store and building it into a business had been destroyed. She didn't want to come here, to Magnolia Cove. She wanted to leave and set out on her own. Start her own bakery, but Lori Lou begged her. She pleaded with Becky to give her one more chance."

"One more chance that there baker blew," Mattie said.

I dipped my head in agreement. "Sounds like Becky Ray was pretty ticked off about the whole thing."

"We'd almost been arrested in the last town," Collinsworth said quietly. "Once the dust clears about Lori Lou's death and the murderer is convicted, Becky Ray will move on. She won't sell to the witch mafia anymore."

"Because there's nothing to sell." I started the mixer and stepped back, watching the paddle churn the ingredients. "Collinsworth?"

"Hmm?"

"Do you think Becky Ray was angry at Lori Lou enough that she murdered her?"

The rabbit hopped three feet in the air. "Of course not. Becky Ray would never have killed her sister."

I hitched a shoulder. "I don't know. She doesn't seem too upset by her death."

"Everyone grieves differently."

"She also didn't seem surprised her sister was murdered."

"The people we do business with are dangerous. Becky Ray always told Lori Lou that one day she would get herself killed by working with those folks."

"Yet she continued to work with her sister, too."

"They loved one another."

I clicked my tongue. Something wasn't right. No shocker there. Nothing had been right about this whole deal to begin with.

"Where did Lori Lou live?" I fished lip gloss from my purse.

"With Becky Ray."

I stopped. Confused. My gaze slowly ticked to Collinsworth. "You said you couldn't return to your house. Didn't you say that? You had to stay with me. Why can't you return to the house where Becky is?"

Collinsworth worried his little paws. He was rubbing them so hard I thought he might rub the fur slap off.

"Collinsworth," I warned. "Tell me. What is it about Becky that you're so afraid of."

"Okay," he blurted out. "You're right. I think Becky Ray killed Lori Lou. But I couldn't say anything."

"Why not, tasty treat?" Mattie said.

"Because." He deflated onto the counter. The rabbit placed his head in his paws. It was such a human gesture my chest tightened. "Because Becky swore she would kill me if I said anything."

THIRTEEN

"**W**hy would Becky Ray kill you?"

I waited for what seemed forever before the rabbit spoke. "She swore that if I—"

A rap came from the front of the building. My gaze shot to Collinsworth and Mattie.

"Y'all expecting anyone?"

Both animals shook their heads.

"Who is it?"

The rabbit sighed. "Probably one of Lori Lou's affected, returning for more pie."

My eyelids flared wide. "You're kidding."

Collinsworth shook his head. "No, of course not. I never joke. I'm too much of a gentleman to do so."

Right.

"What do we do?"

"Ignore it and focus on getting the cookies ready. It's all we can do."

I pointed at him. "We're not finished with this conversation."

"I didn't expect we were."

I stared blankly at the mixer. "What happens next?"

"Go to the big cabinet by the door and bring back the purple jar. It's stoppered with cork. You can't miss it."

I did as he asked and slid it over the counter to him.

"Careful!" he snapped. "Without this, we won't be able to break the spell."

"Okay, sure. A little pixie dust in there?"

Collinsworth unstoppered the bottle. A white curl hissed from the neck of the glass. The rabbit inhaled deeply and sighed. "It's better than pixie dust. It's the best stuff on earth."

"What is it?"

His whiskers twitched. "It's a cure-all."

Mattie gasped.

"What?" I said.

Mattie padded over to us. "A cure-all is basically myth. It don't exist. You can't cure every possible problem with one solution."

Collinsworth smiled. "You can't cure all of them, but most of them."

My jaw dropped. "Like cancer?"

He shook his head. "It must be magically related. That's the only way the power works. If it's natural, it won't work. At least that's what I've been told."

I stared at the simple bottle. "But you don't know for fact."

"Do the folks y'all sell the love potions to know about this?" Mattie asked.

"No, of course not. They'd kill us for a potion of such strength. This isn't supposed to exist, remember?"

I took the bottle gently and tipped it to my nose. Notes of rose and cardamon, cinnamon and wood trickled up my nostrils. "Then how does it exist?"

"I told you, Lori Lou and I together, we were magic. This is from our friendship. We worked together and created it. There's not much, but there will still be a touch left over when we're done. Now"—his gaze settled on me—"pour one teaspoon in the mixture. Let the paddle make ten rotations and turn the machine off."

My hand shook as I held the teaspoon beneath the bottle. I exhaled a plume of air. Had to calm my nerves. I closed my eyes, counted to ten, opened them and poured.

The transition to the mixer went perfectly. I counted exactly ten rotations and shut it off.

"What's next?"

"Spoon out cookies."

Mattie scampered into the kitchen.

"Where'd you get to?" I said.

"I wanted to peek at whoever's outside. It's Mayor Battle. Y'all need to hurry."

"Why?" I said, dipping a scoop in the dough.

"Because it looks like an army's stalking down Bubbling Cauldron right behind him."

My voice reached a pitch that could've broken glass. "What? What do you mean an army's coming?"

"The whole town is on their way here," Mattie said.

Maybe Mattie was wrong. I ran to the front room and heeled to a screeching halt. Faces covered the windows. Faces of people I knew—friends, neighbors, countrymen.

Yeah, yeah, I'm being dramatic, I know, but that's about the truth of it.

Folks pressed themselves against the glass like they wanted to eat their way through. As soon as I was spotted—and let's face it, that wasn't hard since the storefront was completely open—fists started pounding.

They wanted in. They wanted pie. Lots of pie.

Their eyes were bloodshot wide, their skin pale, their flesh sweaty. There was a look about them—hungry, starved. As if it wasn't obvious enough, a few folks clawed at the windows.

"Is this an episode of *The Walking Dead*?" It felt like it. I was just waiting for Rick to show up and start hacking his way through the crowd.

I stopped the thought as soon as it started. It wasn't polite to think of folks I cared about as zombies.

I rushed to the kitchen. "We need to get those cookies baking now. Before someone breaks through."

Collinsworth jumped to action. I'd never seen the rabbit move so fast. He helped me scoop dough onto sheets. I threw it into the warm oven. We scooped and plopped twenty more dough mounds onto another smooth pan. The kitchen had two ovens. We slid the next batch in. By the time it was cooking good, the first batch was done.

"Mattie, grab a towel and fan them cool."

Mattie, bless her heart, did exactly as I asked. Without complaint, the cat nabbed a towel and did her best to fan the cookies.

"Y'all realize I don't have thumbs."

"You're doing an amazing job. I'll get you fish-flavored treats when this is all over."

She shivered with pleasure. "Oh, I haven't had any of those in ages." Mattie worked double time to cool the cookies.

That's how we did it. Scoop, bake, cool. After about forty minutes, I slumped onto a stool. Mattie and Collinsworth deflated too. We were exhausted. The sun was barely streaking the sky.

I smiled at the pile of cookies on the tray. "You think that's enough?"

"It's all we have," Collinsworth said. "I counted three hundred. Should be enough to help those affected."

I glanced toward the front. "No one's broken the glass yet."

"It's only a matter of time. We need to get these into their mouths before it happens," he said.

A knock sounded from the back door. Great. They'd gotten tired of trying to break in the front and had decided the rear would be a better entrance.

"Open up, it's Garrick Young."

A wave of relief washed over me. "Thank goodness."

I snapped the lock off and heaved open the door. Garrick towered over me, his face a deep dark scowl that reminded me more of a black hole than actual flesh.

"Why is there a mob out front?"

I clicked my tongue. Oh, this was going to be so good. I'd tried to tell him, but Garrick hadn't listened.

"There's a mob because the pies Lori Lou sold were all filled with giving potions. She didn't have the spell worked out right, and now we've got a bunch of addicts on our hands. Addicts in withdrawal."

His face paled. His eyes widened. Garrick swallowed. His Adam's apple bobbed.

"Don't worry, I've got cookies that will help. But I need you, Sheriff Young, to stop them from mowing me down when I open the front door."

He raked his fingers down his face. "Okay. Let's do this."

"Rabbit, I'm going to need your help, too."

Garrick stepped into the front room, took one look at the faces smashed against the windows and paused. "I'm going through the back."

"What?"

"They'll trample each other if we open this door. Too much of a bottleneck for it to work. I'll pull them from the door and then you can go outside with your basket of goodies."

Sounded like a better plan than mine. "Okay."

Garrick left. After about a minute I heard him yelling at people, but it didn't appear that anyone was listening. Their faces were still eyeing me like I was a T-bone steak and they were stranded on a deserted island.

"Come on, Garrick," I said.

Finally folks peeled from the glass. It was slow and painful, like a little kid afraid of ripping off a bandage.

"About time."

Finally, when there was enough room for me to open the door and stand without being suffocated, I quietly turned the lock and glanced over my shoulder. Only Mattie stood in the room with me.

"Collinsworth, you little chicken, get your butt over here."

The rabbit hopped out from behind a chair. "But I'm so small and delicate. I can't be manhandled. My fur. It's so white and beautiful."

My gaze tipped to the ceiling. I shook my head and sighed. "Get. Over. Here."

His whiskers twitched as he hopped. "Promise no one will harm me?"

"I'll harm you if you don't grab your little basket and help. Not come on."

I pushed the door slowly, slightly afraid that if I moved too quickly, the Thanksgiving apocalypse would descend on me. I stepped around the crowd, knowing that my biggest ally in this was Garrick. If I was next to him, nothing would hurt me.

Except Axel twisting my heart with his absence.

Okay, I really needed to focus on the now.

I sneaked around the crowd and padded to Garrick, who had his arms out and his mouth drawn to a grim line.

He pointed to the basket. "Everyone just take one. You get one cookie. That's all. Move slow."

I held out the basket as folks greedily took a cookie. Most of them shoved the discs in their mouths immediately. A few nibbled the edges slowly, savoring it.

My eyes nearly bugged from my head when I saw Betty among the knot of folks. My heart jumped in my chest. She needed a cookie in a bad way.

I waved and called, "Betty!" I looked like I was bringing in a plane for landing. "Betty!"

She shuffled toward me. I still had a few left when another voice rang out in the morning.

"Everyone stop eating!"

Garrick scowled. We turned in unison to the sound. Not far off stood a small woman wearing a bright red suit. She had a short blonde bob, thick legs and her hands on her hips.

She raised a sheet of paper. "Give me all your cookies! I've got a warrant for them."

Anger gushed in my chest. No way was this little woman wearing a garish suit going to ruin the one shot I had at keeping this town safe. "Who are you?"

"I'm Farinas Harrell."

"Carmen's attorney," Garrick said.

She clomped over on cherry-colored heels. She waved the paper in my face like it was the flag and I should've been saluting it. The only thing I wanted to salute was her with my middle finger.

Yes, y'all, I was pretty upset about the whole situation.

"I've got a warrant for these cookies. Hand 'em over." Farinas snatched discs from addicts' hands and stuffed them in her purse.

"Wait a minute." I yanked them right out. "You can't do this. These people need them."

She shoved a finger under my nose. "I can do this. I have a warrant. Every last one of these is mine. They're now evidence in the case the police have against my client."

I stood dumbstruck. "Why?" She grabbed the cookie I held limply. "Why are you taking them? These people…" I didn't want to come right out and say they were addicts, that they needed these cookies. It sounded so stupid.

"These people are sick. There's medicine in them," was all I managed.

Farinas continued plucking and stashing. "That's what I aim to prove. That Lori Lou was killed for reasons other than jealousy. These are evidence."

I shot Garrick a pleading look. "You have to help me."

He lowered his badge. "I can't. She has a warrant." He said it so limply, like he was resigned to the same fate as I was.

"But Garrick."

He squeezed my shoulder. "There's nothing I can do."

"You can help me round them up," she snapped.

I wanted to punch her. I raked my fingers down my face. "Look, you're helping my cousin. I'm trying to help these people."

"Warrant," was all she said. "Look, if you're going to stop me, I'll have you arrested. I've got the law on my side, honey. The law and my handbag."

"Which you're stuffing full of cookies."

She snatched one from Mayor Battle before he could take a bite. "Evidence."

I ran back to Garrick. "Cordelia ate the pie." It was the only ace I had left.

His gaze darkened. He shuffled his weight and hung his head in shame. "I can't do anything."

There was only one choice. I rushed over to Collinsworth and pulled him to the side. "Do you think there's enough potion left to make one more batch?"

The rabbit worried his paws. "Possibly. If you stretch it."

I nibbled my bottom lip. If Farinas was here to inspect the entire store, I needed to get that bottle and get the heck out before she saw me.

"Cover for me," I said to Mattie.

"Sugar, ain't nothin' I would love more."

Mattie scampered up to Farinas and jumped in her purse. The attorney teetered on her heels.

"What in the...? Get out of my bag, you stupid cat!"

It was official. I did not like Farinas. Anyone who dared to call Mattie stupid was at the bottom of my I-like-you list.

Farinas stumbled back, managing to turn completely away from me. I sprinted into the building, heading straight to the kitchen. I flung open the cabinet door and searched for the bottle.

Collinsworth had placed it on the center shelf, right in front. I'd seen him do it. There had been lots of other bottles in there too. But now the entire cabinet was empty.

I sucked air. Holy crap. While we'd been outside, someone had walked into the Sweet Witch and stolen the one shot I had to save this town.

FOURTEEN

Farinas left the street a little while later. I scowled at her
backside, wishing she'd never arrived in town.

Betty leaned her head against a tree. She stared as if trying to
figure out a way to eat it.

"Need a fork and knife?"

Her gaze swept from my feet to my crown. "Very funny."

"Let's get you home." I pinched her elbow and started to drag her.

She yanked out. "I feel great."

"You're sweating. Your eyes are glassy." I put my knuckles to her
forehead. "You're hot. Let's get you home."

Mattie and Collinsworth approached. "We're taking Betty home."

"You do not look good," Mattie said.

"I feel great. All I need is a little honeysuckle wine, my pipe and I'll
be fine," Betty said.

She took a step. Her knees wobbled. I braced her in my arms.
"Let's go."

I managed to get her home and put her in bed. She closed her eyes
and mumbled, "My pipe. I need my pipe."

"Not right now you don't. You'll burn down the house. Probably
fall asleep with it cindering."

She stared at me with fever-bright eyes. "I would not."

Tylenol was my first thought. "I'll be back. Mattie, stay with Betty."

"You got it, sugar." Mattie curled up beside Betty's pillow.

I left the room and knocked on Cordelia's door. No answer. I raked my fingers through my hair and headed into the kitchen, where all the medications were kept. I found the Tylenol, shook two into my hand and headed back upstairs.

I gave the dose to Betty along with some water, sat on her bed and waited until she dozed off, which was about ten minutes later.

I scraped my fingernails down my face. For some reason the twinge of pain made me feel better. I found a thermometer in the bathroom and took Betty's temperature.

She had a fever. The Tylenol would take care of it, but I was worried. I had to do something. I called Cordelia and Amelia but didn't get an answer.

I racked my brain until it hit me. The bottle holding the potion was missing. Who would've stolen it?

The name hit me like a monster truck sliding in mud. I found Collinsworth in my bedroom. "Where's Becky Ray's house?"

"I don't know."

"You do know. If fact, we never finished our conversation from earlier. We'll do that in the car. Come on."

I hardly ever used my vehicle, but it needed to be run. I grabbed Collinsworth by the collar and practically had to drag him to the door before he stopped trying to dig his paws in the floor.

"She'll kill me."

"I'll protect you. Don't worry. I'm a head witch. I can make seriously cool stuff happen with my mind."

The rabbit finally stopped fighting. I picked him up and entered Betty's room. Mattie blinked at me. "I'm on my way to Becky Ray's. We shouldn't be gone too long. I'd call you, but you can't use a cell phone."

"Never tried," she said.

"I'll text Cordelia and Amelia and let them know what's going on."

I texted my cousins that Betty was running a fever and in bed. I asked Cordelia how she was feeling and slid the phone in my front pocket.

I hoisted Collinsworth onto my hip.

"I have some dignity," he sniffed.

"Not anymore."

I fastened his seat belt, slid into the driver's seat and fired up the engine. "Where are we going?"

"I'm not telling you."

I turned to face the rabbit and plastered on my most evil look. "Listen to me, rabbit, if you don't tell me what I want to know, I will tell Sheriff Garrick that you are personally responsible for the giving potion mess. I will make sure he sticks you in a dark, nasty cell and denies you hot tea. For the rest of your life."

The rabbit shuddered. "You wouldn't."

"Try me, Cottontail."

Collinsworth paused. His nose twitched as he stared out the window. "It's on Eastwitch."

"Perfect."

It was a couple of minutes away. Not far. It wasn't like Magnolia Cove was some booming metropolis. Most anywhere you wanted to go was within a few clicks of somewhere else.

"It's the green house."

I slid the vehicle to a stop and stared. We'd arrived, which was great. But what was I going to do now? It's wasn't like I could just break and enter in the middle of the day.

Couldn't I?

"What's her phone number?"

Collinsworth blinked rapid fire my way. "I don't know."

"Nasty little cell."

He shot off numbers like a Gatling gun. I thumbed them into my phone and pressed the call button.

A few seconds later Becky Ray answered. "Hello?"

"This is Sergeant Ritter at the police department. We need you to come down and identify a batch of magical cookies. We're investigating them."

Her breath came out raspy. "What sort of magical cookies?"

"The kind that look like they might be a real problem for Magnolia Cove."

She paused. "I'll be right there."

So either Becky Ray was going to run as far away from town as she could get, or she'd be nosy enough to figure out what was going on. My hope was on the fact that she'd want to know what the police could have that might get her in trouble.

She seemed the nosy type.

Within seconds Becky was out the door and huffing and puffing her way toward the station.

"This should buy us some time. Ten minutes there. Five minutes for the mess to be straightened out, ten minutes back." Collinsworth had sunk into his seat, hiding himself from Becky. "What's wrong? Why is Becky going to kill you?"

"She told me that if I ever mentioned the illegal potions to anyone, she'd take care of me. I told you."

"Ah." My head fell back. I stretched my neck. My muscles were knotted and tight after the night I'd had. Lord, I needed sleep. But I needed the potion first.

"And I basically told Becky Ray I know all about it—what with the black car and the trash bags."

"So now she's definitely going to kill me."

He tried to jump in his seat but got tangled in the belt. "Sit your britches down. Come on. Help me check the house. We need that potion."

The rabbit calmed enough for me to unravel him from the strap, tuck him under my arm and make my way to the house.

"There's a spare key in a rock by the back door."

We headed around back. I craned my neck this way and that, making sure no one was watching. I did not need to get busted breaking into this house. Of course the rabbit could say I was helping him move some things.

Wow. It was amazing how deviant my mind became when I gave it the chance. Must've been the Betty Craple in me.

We entered and I set Collinsworth down. "We need to find that potion."

He shivered. "I don't know where Becky would put it."

"Let's start in the kitchen."

I rummaged through cupboards and drawers. It hadn't been that long since it had been taken this morning, she couldn't have put it too far away.

I hoped. Half of Magnolia Cove might still need it. I know Betty did.

It felt like an invisible hand squeezed my heart. The thought of Betty being sick because of a stupid potion made anger burn in my veins.

"It's not here," I said, nearly slamming a cupboard shut. "Bedroom."

I followed Collinsworth as he hopped through the house. He took me to a bedroom with off-white walls and sparse furnishings. A few porcelain figurines sat on the dresser. Angel babies with fat cheeks.

"This is Becky's room?"

He nodded.

"I'm surprised those aren't tiny devils instead of angels. She's not exactly the warm and cuddly type."

He didn't say anything. I stepped in and started riffling through drawers. "Clothes, clothes and more clothes." I moved to the closet. A series of shoeboxes lined the back wall.

"What's this?"

I pulled one out and lifted the lid. It was filled with cards. Recipes. For potions. Stacks and stacks of them all tucked neatly away and filed in a place where no one would look for them.

Collinsworth hopped over. "What are they?"

"You said Lori Lou devised the potions."

"She did. They were all her recipes."

"Then what're these?" I lowered the box so he could see.

"I...I don't know. Perhaps I could figure it out over a cup of Earl Grey."

"No Earl Grey. Why are these in here? Why would Becky Ray have them? Look, this one is the pie recipe Carmen said was stolen and here's another for a giving potion."

Collinsworth's nose twitched. "I don't know. I told you the truth. Lori Lou created the spells. These aren't hers. It's different."

Gears in my brain clicked at high speed. "What if Becky Ray had her own ideas for the business, and those ideas didn't work out with what Lori Lou wanted?"

The rabbit's eyes narrowed. "You mean they wanted separate things?"

"Was it enough to kill over?"

"I don't know."

I tucked the card in the box and closed the lid. "That's what we need to find out."

The sound of a door opening came from the other side of the house. Collinsworth and I shot bug eyes at each other.

There was no way Becky Ray was back so quickly. We'd only been in the house a few minutes.

"Lori Lou's room. Quick."

I followed him as silently as possible down the hall and through an opening. I quietly shut the door as I heard Becky Ray rummaging around the kitchen. Good. Maybe she would cook up something to eat and the extra sound would help us.

I scanned Lori Lou's room. Beside her full-size bed covered in a pink lacy bedspread lay a smaller matchbox bed. The word COLLINSWORTH was burned into the wooden headboard. It was so small and cute my heart squeezed.

I almost felt sorry for the little lying rabbit.

"The window," he whispered.

Risking a moment to snoop, I opened Lori Lou's nightstand drawer. There was a faded pink rose, some scraps of paper and tissues. One of the scraps looked familiar. I snatched it up. Written on the back was a phone number. I slid it into my pocket.

"What are you doing?" Collinsworth said. "We have to hurry."

I tucked the shoebox tightly under my armpit and crossed to the window. I snapped the lock and pushed.

The frame was painted shut.

Now why did people do that? Every freaking apartment I'd ever lived in had all the stupid windows painted shut. Could the painters not take a second with their work and not seal the stupid windows? It totally irked me. Like, if you wanted to annoy me, come to my house and paint the windows closed. We'd never be friends.

Just kidding.

Sighing and needing something to boost my brain into overdrive, I dug into my pocket, pulled out a bag of jelly beans and popped every single hot cinnamon-flavored bean into my mouth.

It was something about cinnamon and heat that got my brain working. I closed my eyes. I had extra power that needed burning off anyway.

If I didn't use my magic, I got headaches that meant my power was building up. My ability was like a pressure cooker. If I didn't release some of the energy every once in a while, the force would kill me.

Like I said, I had magic to spare. I thought of my finger as a blade and scraped it around the window. The paint crackled and snapped. My heartbeat launched into my throat. My palms were slick with sweat, and my stomach was a jumbling mess.

"Hurry," Collinsworth said. "She's coming."

My eyes snapped open. I gave the window one good shove. It shot up so fast I thought it might explode through the roof.

I jumped out, landing softly on the grass. I reached back to grab Collinsworth. I slipped my hands underneath him and tugged.

His jacket caught on a splinter jutting out of the wood. I pulled, but the splinter was strong.

"She's coming! Hurry," he said.

I pulled, but he was not budging. "Take off the coat."

"I can't. I won't. It's my signature," he said.

"You have to," I hissed. "Hurry."

Like, I didn't know what Becky Ray was doing in there, but it sounded like she was stomping through the house wearing bricks. The structure rumbled as she made her way down the hall.

"You have to."

I heard the footsteps stop. It sounded like they were outside the door.

"I won't," he whispered.

I hit his jacket with a splash of magic. The coat flung off him, and I yanked Collinsworth out the window. I reached for the jacket as the door opened.

There wasn't time. I couldn't grab the jacket and run to my car, so I did the only thing I could.

I left the jacket for Becky Ray to find. She would know Collinsworth had been there.

With the shoebox under one arm and Collinsworth tucked beneath the other, I sprinted to the car. I unlocked the door, stuck the rabbit on my lap and streaked down the street.

After a moment he sulkily shifted to the passenger side. "She'll come after us, you know," he said. "There'll be no escape."

FIFTEEN

*B*y the time the rabbit and I returned to the house, Cordelia and Amelia had arrived. Cordelia didn't look good, but she wasn't nearly as bad as Betty.

My cousin lay bundled on the couch. "I don't know what's wrong with me, but I want more pie."

I checked her temperature. It was elevated. "Let me get you some Tylenol."

I bumped into Amelia in the kitchen. She took one look at me and gaped. I still had Collinsworth tucked under my arm. I was worried the rabbit would run away and I would still need his help.

"Why are you naked?" Amelia said to him.

The rabbit glared at me. "Because someone had to go snooping."

Amelia shot me a confused look. "What's going on? Betty's never sick."

I cringed. "We've got a serious problem. She's going through withdrawals from the pie. The withdrawals are so bad that she and a whole bunch of other people could die. The one shot I had at saving folks was ruined by Farinas, aka Nancy Grace wannabe."

I sank onto a chair. "How's Betty?"

"She asked the name of the purple dragon."

I frowned. "What purple dragon?"

"The one that was in her room."

"Oh Lord, she's delirious." I shouldered my purse. "Watch Collinsworth." I headed to the front door.

"Where are you going?"

"To the police station to get those cookies back."

I headed out and had to stop myself from crumbling onto the porch and bursting into tears. This was hard, y'all. Carmen's attorney was trying to help, but she'd just ruined the town's chances of getting healthy. I could only hope the folks who had a bite or two of the cookies had eaten enough to keep them from going into severe withdrawals.

My mind flashed to Axel—to his blue eyes, dark hair, strong arms that could wrap me up and make all the bad go away. He always, always had a solution. I was swimming in the middle of the ocean. Sharks were circling, and the only thing between me and them was a stick and an inflatable raft with a leak.

Seriously, that's how I felt. I needed help. I needed Garrick to listen.

My phone rang. I snatched it from my purse and was relieved when I saw the number flashing on the screen.

"Hello?"

"How're things going?"

I bit back tears. "It's horrible, Rufus. I had the town cured. Me. I had them cured, but then Farinas Harrell appeared and screwed everything up."

"Sounds like her."

I laughed bitterly. Some of the tension melted from my shoulders. It was sick and wrong that talking to Rufus made me feel better. It should've been Axel I was confiding in.

"I ran the plate you gave me."

"You're not a cop."

He chuckled. "You'd be surprised the access I have. I ran it, and yes, absolutely shady characters were traced to it."

"So bad guys buying love potions."

"More than likely."

I had nothing else to say. There wasn't anything that could help me right now.

"What do you need?" he said.

"A miracle," I said bitterly. "The wizards and witches who can help are either gone or sick. Axel's not here, Betty's in bed. Those are the most powerful people I know."

He paused. "Wrong. You know someone else."

"Who?" Oh no. He meant— "You mean you?"

"You don't have to sound so surprised. I know magic, and I know how to help with potions."

"You can't come here. No one will let you. Besides, I think most of the cookies were eaten."

"Are you sure?"

"No. I don't know."

"Calm down," he soothed. "Even if I can't get in, I can still direct you."

"How?"

"My mother's house might have something that can assist."

I cringed. Rufus's mother had traded gifts for personal treasures. I'd only been outside it, but the place freaked me out.

"I don't know. Let me think about it. People might be okay."

"I'm here if you need me."

The words twisted my gut. Rufus, the evil Rufus was here to help me and Axel wasn't. How ironic was that?

I needed to think. I needed time. I needed to breathe. "I'll call you if anything changes."

"Don't hesitate."

"Rufus?"

"Pepper?"

"Don't be sarcastic. I'm trying to say something nice."

"I like how you think me saying your name is dripping with sarcasm. Did you ever stop to think that maybe I just like saying your name?"

"No. I didn't because I don't think of you as human."

Wow. That was so mean. Rufus had started out as a horrible person, but he'd gotten better. Or at least our interactions had reached more of a civilized nature.

"You realize I do have feelings," Rufus said.

I closed my eyes. "I'm sorry. I've been stressed."

"I can tell, which is why I'm saying that if you need me, I'm here. My mother may have something in her house that will stop all this. Or at least get everyone through the withdrawals so that the giving spell is broken."

I nibbled my bottom lip. "I'll call you back."

"I'll be here."

"And Rufus?"

"Yes?"

"Thank you."

"Pepper, you are very welcome."

I pushed down my bag of jumbled feelings and marched to the police station. When I entered, Farinas Harrell, the woman who ruined my morning, was talking to Carmen. I couldn't hear what they were saying. Must've been some sort of magic to shield their attorney/client privilege.

I found Garrick in his office. His gaze lifted to me, and I could see regret immediately fill his eyes.

"Where are the cookies?"

He tipped his head, avoiding me. "In evidence."

"What does Farinas think she's going to do with them? Be Nancy Drew as well as Nancy Grace?"

He ground his teeth. "Pepper, I couldn't do anything. There was a warrant."

"Betty is ill."

"So is half the town."

I sank against the wall. "They are?"

Garrick rubbed his jaw. "I'm getting reports. People are sick in bed. Fevers, chills."

"We need those cookies."

He opened his drawer and pulled out something wrapped in a napkin. "I've got two. That's it."

"How's that going to help?"

He glared at me as if I was denser than a rock. "One for Betty. One for Cordelia."

I sank into a chair. "Thank goodness. I may be able to help with the others. I've been in touch with—" I didn't want to say *Rufus* because Garrick disliked him as much as the next person.

"You've been in touch with…?" He was waiting.

"A wizard. Someone who might be able to assist. I don't know how long it will take."

"Get on it," Garrick said.

I rose.

"Pepper, if there's anything you need from me, don't hesitate."

"Okay. Thank you."

I left with the cookies stashed in my purse. Thank goodness. Two people down, only a hundred or so left to go. Let's hope Rufus was right and the answers could be found in his mother's old house.

BETTY WAS DELIRIOUS. She gazed at me with bright, glassy eyes and kept mumbling about the purple dragon. His flesh was scorching.

"Give me a cookie."

Amelia unwrapped the napkin and handed one to me. I raised Betty in my arms. She fought but I cooed to her.

"Just take a few bites of this."

Her head tipped back. "Is it the purple dragon?"

"Yes." What else was I going to say?

She munched hungrily. Amelia handed me a glass of water. Betty drank like she'd been lost in the desert for days. When I was convinced the little bit of cookie had reached her stomach, I lowered her back to the pillow.

"Every time she wakes, make her eat some cookie until it's all gone."

Amelia nodded. "I'll give it to Cordelia. She's not nearly as bad off."

"Good." I shrank. "I wonder."

"What?"

I studied Amelia. No fever, no delirium. "Why didn't you get sick?"

She shrugged. "Could be natural immunity. I've been given a potion before."

"You have? When?"

The usual light in her eyes faded. "Never mind."

I took the hint that our conversation was finished. "I have to go. I'm sorry. I want to stay."

Amelia tugged her hair. "Don't worry. I've got someone coming over to help."

"Who?"

She swatted the air. "Just a friend. No big deal."

Which meant it was a big deal, but I wasn't about to ask. It wasn't my business. But I still wanted to know. I shot Amelia a questioning look.

"It's Dicky Downy, but don't tell anyone." She huffed in annoyance. "People have opinions about him."

"That's what I'd gathered, but he has a thing for you."

"We were always friends in high school. The timing never worked out."

I clicked my tongue. "Well, I hope this time it does work."

She nodded. For having a guy coming over, she didn't look excited about it. Strange. "Maybe so."

Collinsworth hopped in. He'd pinned a yellow dish towel over his shoulders.

"Who are you supposed to be, Super Bunny? No, wait. I've got it, you're Bunnicula."

"I am naked thanks to you, so I had to do what I could to regain some decency."

"Not sure that's decent, but come on, you can redeem yourself by coming with me."

"To do what?"

"See how we can minimize the effects of the spell. All the best witches and wizards are either sick or missing in action. It's up to us."

"I've always wanted to be a hero," he said proudly.

"Great. Now's your chance."

I grabbed Mattie from my bedroom. I gave Hugo a pat on the head. "Watch the family. I need you to stay here and protect them."

"From what, sugar?" Mattie said.

"I don't know. Becky Ray. Someone else? You okay with that, Hugo?"

In my head the answer popped with clarity, *Yes, Mama.*

Great. We were all set. The three of us tromped downstairs and out the front door, where we were met by Licky and Mint.

"Pepper, where are y'all going?" Mint said, gazing at my animal caravan.

Oh no. Tricky. Should I tell them? Doing so would almost certainly mean they would want to come along. They were my aunts, after all. I loved them, and honestly, they'd known my mother all their lives and could probably tell me anything I wanted about her.

But at the same time they exhaled chaos. It followed them everywhere. The cooked turkey was case in point. If I brought them with me to Melbalean Mayes's house, the place would probably explode— with me in it.

"Um. Well."

"People are sick, Pepper," Licky said, throwing a long strand of silky hair over her shoulder.

"So sick," Mint said. "I'm beginning to feel like us healthy folks need to stick together so we don't catch it."

"My throat keeps threatening to tickle," Licky said.

Mint pulled a pill from her pocket. "Take this. It's an antihistamine."

"That should help. Post-nasal drip is terrible."

"All the leaves in the air," Mint said.

I frowned. "They've fallen and are off the trees."

"Well, it's something," Mint said.

The three of us stared at one another. Mint rocked on her heels while Licky picked at a fingernail.

"You look like you're going someplace important," Mint said.

"We want to help," Licky said.

I heaved out a large breath. "Look, I know you want to help. It's just…" My throat constricted. I couldn't say it. The words wouldn't come. I couldn't tell my aunts that I was afraid they'd totally screw up what I was doing and that they'd make the mess a thousand times worse.

It was just so impolite. With everything else that had happened, I didn't want to alienate anyone. Let's face it, I needed all the allies I could get.

I pulled my hair over one shoulder. "I'm going to Melbalean Mayes's house."

Their eyes widened. "Whatever for?" Mint said.

"The house may hold something that will help us cure everyone. I've got to take the chance. Betty and Cordelia are going to get better; I've already made sure of that. But I can't say the same for everyone else."

Mint and Licky exchanged a look. Finally Licky smacked her lips. "Well, what're we waiting for then? Let's go break into an abandoned home."

SIXTEEN

$\mathcal{W}$e reached Melbalean Mayes's house. The place looked part haunted house, part condemned building.

This was going to be awesome.

"So what do we do now?" Mint said.

My stomach sank. I'd been dreading this part. "I have to call Rufus. He's going to walk me through it."

The glance Mint and Licky exchanged was priceless. It looked like atomic bombs had exploded in both their brains.

All I had to do was wait for it.

Licky wrung a finger in her ear. "Did you say Rufus?"

I sighed. "Yes, ma'am, I did. He's been— I almost hate to say it, but he's been helping me."

"Of course he has," Mint said.

I stopped. "What's that mean?"

My aunts exchanged another look. Finally Mint said, "It doesn't mean anything other than he thinks you're his friend."

"Remember when he was here on Halloween?" Licky said.

"He went to you, Pepper," Mint said.

"Because he wants to be your friend," Licky said.

I examined their expressions for a hint they were hiding something, but I didn't see anything. Something unsaid filled the air. It bothered me.

I shot Collinsworth and Mattie a look. "Stay with my aunts. I'll be right back."

I gave myself some distance and dialed the number. Licky and Mint's reactions to my relationship with Rufus had been loaded with tension, and I completely understood why.

"I'm here," was all I said when Rufus answered.

"At the house?"

"Yes."

"Okay, once you're inside, go to the basement."

Why did it always have to be the basement? Couldn't anything of magic be found in another room? But no, for some reason it always had to be the creepiest room ever that magical objects were stashed and stored in.

"Okay, what happens when I'm in there?"

"There will be a rack filled with jars and bottles."

Sounded easy. Maybe this would be a piece of cake. "Will I find what I need there?"

"No."

Crap. "Let me get to the basement."

Licky was zapping the back door when I walked up. She pushed it open with a finger. "We're in, Pepper."

"Officially breaking and entering," Mint said proudly.

"With our niece," Licky added enthusiastically.

They switched on some lights. The home was decorated with doilies and velvet furniture. Little boy figurines were perched on most of the surfaces. Sometimes the boy sat, sometimes he fished. At other times he reached for something.

I never understood people's fascination with figurines. Especially since we were talking about Melbalean Mayes. She'd been into some really dark stuff. The fact that she'd sprinkled sweet little boys around her house managed to creep me out.

I shivered. "Okay, we're in. I'm heading to the basement."

Mint and Licky moved ahead. The place was eerie, y'all. It

wouldn't have surprised me if a skeleton jumped from a closet and grabbed me. My aunts didn't notice my unease. They walked around flipping lights and making a ton of noise.

"Pretty dusty here," Mint said.

"Let me clean these cobwebs," Licky said.

By the time I reached the bottom of the basement stairs, Licky had a broom in her hand and was clearing the ceiling of webs, while Mint was dusting surfaces with an old rag.

It certainly paid to have aunts who were witches. Finally, Licky said, "Oh, let's just do this the old-fashioned way."

My aunts smiled at each other. They placed an arm atop the other like genies, bobbed their heads and in a flash of light, the place was sparkling.

"Hopefully the dust wasn't magical and we needed it," I said.

Mint squeezed my arms. "Don't worry, if we have to get it back, it's no problem."

"Great," I said without enthusiasm. I pressed the phone to my ear. "I'm in the basement. Oh, I see the rack of potions."

"Good," Rufus said. "Do you see the third rack down?"

"Yes."

"Push the potions aside. Behind them there should be a joint in the wall. Press it."

"What will happen?"

"A skeleton hand will pop out and grab you."

"I knew it! The place is booby-trapped."

Rufus chuckled softly. "That's not going to happen. The wall will open to a small hole. There should be a box inside."

"Okay. Hold on."

Mattie and Collinsworth approached. "Sugar, you need us to do anything?" the cat said.

I shook my head. "Just stand back."

I parted the bottles. Glass clinked. Thick liquids gurgled in the glass. The faint smell of earth trickled up my nose. I hoped that was the worst smell I encountered in this mess.

I saw an outline in the wall as if the plaster had been cut. I pressed it, and sure enough, a small portion of the surface was hinged. A square sprang open. I pulled a small porcelain boy from the hideaway.

"You've got to be kidding." The boy wore a blue coat and shorts and was holding a ukulele. His strawberry-colored mouth was shaped in a perfect bow.

There wasn't a box with some sort of ingredient aside. This must've been Rufus's idea of a joke.

I gritted my teeth and plucked the phone from the table. "What am I supposed to do with a blue boy?"

"What?"

"You heard me. There isn't a box. It's a porcelain figurine. Are you kidding me? I've got an entire town that needs help and you're giving me this?"

"The boy is made of the powder."

"What's he saying?" Mint said.

I palmed the microphone. "He says the ingredient is the boy."

"Give me the phone."

I dropped it into my aunt's extended hand. "Rufus, this is Mint Craple. What do I need to do?"

While she spoke to him, my aunt walked around grabbing this bottle and that. She found three different sizes of mortars and pestles and set them out. After about five minutes she said, "And that's it? That should do it?"

Mint listened. Finally she spoke. "Okay. We've got it. We'll call you back if we have any more questions. Thank you."

She thumbed off the phone and handed it to me. I dropped it in my purse.

"All hands on deck," she said. We circled her. Mint inspected us from head to toe—yes, even the rabbit.

"Y'all, we have a lot of work to do. I'm going to give each of you specific tasks. Rabbit, I need you at the smallest mortar and pestle. Mattie, I'm going to have you adding ingredients to the cauldron as I hand them off while the three of us witches mix and grind."

Never had I seen one of my aunts take such amazing initiative. Personally I didn't know what to think. It was pretty impressive.

Mint broke the blue boy in half and dumped the parts in two separate bowls. Licky and I started grinding while Mint found a cauldron, filled it with water and got it heating over her witch's fire.

"What did Rufus tell you?" I said.

She read labels and measured ingredients. "He told me this wasn't any different from a basic curing spell."

"Oh," Licky said, "we've performed tons of those."

We stood lined up at the counter. "You have? You've worked curing spells before?"

Mint laughed. "Yep. When our mother owned the town pharmacy, she made us come in and learn every day after school. We had to mix, grind, measure."

"All that good stuff," Licky said.

"I forget that Betty is a healer," I said.

Licky snorted. "No one could blame you there. If she was warm and cuddly, it might be easier to remember."

"Hard as nails," Mint said.

My gaze darted between them. "But you two..." I stopped. What was about to expel from my mouth sounded so rude.

"But we're what?" Mint said, surprise in her voice.

"Chaos witches?" Licky said. "We'd end up breaking someone's leg before we had a chance to cure them?"

"Something like that," I mumbled. See? It sounded plain old rude.

"For your information, when we worked with Betty, our powers were better," Mint said.

"More controllable," Licky added. "Is that a word? Controllable?"

"Yes," I said, embarrassed. "But don't get me wrong. It's not like I think things explode everywhere you go."

"But they do," Mint said.

I eyed the potion we were working on.

Licky patted my shoulder. "Curing is different for us. For some reason it keeps the chaos in check."

"Yes," Mint said. "So much that it was at Betty's shop when we met our husbands."

The bottom fell out. "I'm sorry. What?"

"Our husbands? You know, Amelia's and Cordelia's fathers?" Licky said.

"I just figured they were test-tube babies."

My aunts laughed. "No. Hardly," Mint said. "We got them the hard way. Wait. I mean we had them the hard way."

"It sounds sexual either way," Licky said.

My cheeks burned. I did not need to be having an uncomfortable birds-and-bees discussion with my aunts.

Mint waved dismissively. "I remember the first time Bean walked in the room." She noticed my confusion and smiled. "We all called him Bean because he was so tall—and so funny."

"He was," Licky said.

"We had such fun together. And of course Licky dated Morgan."

Her gaze flashed to me. "He didn't have a cool nickname like Bean. Just Morgan." Licky shot me a conspiratorial look. "The four of us used to have fun. Those were the best times, when we would double date."

The wistful expression on both their faces reminded me of my own great times with Axel.

"Why don't you talk about them? Cordelia and Amelia never mention their dads."

My aunts exchanged a look. Licky took the reins. "Oh well, that would be because they don't know them."

I pressed the pestle into herbs I'd been given. At least, they smelled like herbs. Couldn't been dried eyeballs for all I knew.

"Why don't they know their dads?"

"Well," Mint said, embarrassed. "It's kind of a long story."

"I have time."

"Betty didn't want us to date Morgan and Bean," Licky said.

"Why not? She always seems to want us to be happy."

"They were brothers, for one," Mint said.

"Y'all are sisters," I said.

"Betty said the more we separated in our love lives, the better off we'd be because of the whole chaos thing," Licky explained.

"Oh, okay. I guess that makes sense."

My aunts were quiet. Too quiet. I saw them give side-eyes to each other.

I stopped grinding. "But that's not all, is it? There's something more."

Mint licked her lips. "Yes, there was something more. There was another reason why Betty didn't want us to date Bean and Morgan."

"Which is of course why we ran off and married them," Licky said.

Oh wow. I hadn't expected that.

"Okay. What was it? What's the reason Betty didn't want y'all to marry Bean and Morgan."

"Well..." Mint started.

"It was very simple," Licky said.

"They were different."

Licky eyed her. "But not too different."

"You're right," Mint said. "Just different enough to make a difference."

Oh Lord. I could feel the chaos growing in the room. It was thick pressure. Like when you step outside and realize it's going to rain. You don't know when or how much, but you know at some point the sky is going to open and empty.

That's what Mint's and Licky's burgeoning power felt like. I needed to help them rein it in.

"Your power is building."

Mint laughed uneasily. "Sorry. Sometimes we don't pay attention."

"It's all this talk about our husbands," Licky said.

"Are y'all still married?" I said.

"Oh yes," Licky said. "We love them."

I was tired of playing Round Robin. "So what's the big deal? Why didn't Betty want you with them?"

Mint exhaled. "Because of what they are."

"What are they?"

My aunts exchanged a charged look. Finally Licky licked her lips. "They were sort of like us. A lot of chaos would come into their lives at times when we least expected it."

"I don't understand. Were they witches?"

"They are," Mint said. "But they're half something else."

Fascinating. Lots of halfsies in this town. I was technically only half witch. My father had been completely nonmagical.

I stopped grinding the herbs. "What else were they?"

Licky swallowed. "They were half genie."

My jaw dropped. "You mean they can grant wishes?"

Mint nodded. "Yep. When they weren't screwing them up."

I tucked a strand of hair behind my ear. "So does that mean? Cordelia and Amelia?"

They nodded in unison. Licky spoke. "It means your cousins are part genie."

SEVENTEEN

"My cousins are part genie? Why haven't they told me?"

I stared at the substance I'd ground to a pulp. Mint whisked it away and dropped it in hers. She started grinding. Licky also took an inappropriate interest in the contents of the bowl.

So basically my aunts were avoiding me. Alarm bells blared in my head.

"What's up?" I said.

"Nothing," Mint said.

"Just working this spell," Licky said.

"Is that why neither of you answered my question?"

"Hmm? What question?" Mint said.

"They ain't gonna answer," Mattie said.

"I would concur," Collinsworth stated. "Even though I may not have appropriate clothing, I can still tell when someone is being evasive."

"Thanks, y'all." I put on my best intimidating scowl and cleared my throat. "They don't know, do they?"

Mint glanced up. "Who?"

"Cordelia and Amelia. They have no idea what they are."

Guilty looks shot through the room.

My stomach bottomed out. How could my cousins not know what they were but I did? There was no justice in this world. I didn't want to have this sort of knowledge. Be responsible for knowing that my cousins could grant wishes when they didn't even know it themselves.

"I'm going to tell them," I said.

"No!" my aunts screamed in unison.

I glared at them. "You both need to tell me the story. Right now."

"While we work," Licky said.

"Yes," Mint said. "We have to finish this too."

"I need tea," I said.

Mint whipped up a glass of sweet tea for me. I hadn't mastered the technique of making food and drink appear when I wanted.

There was still so much to learn.

Apparently so, since my aunts were dumping the secret of a lifetime on me.

I dropped some jelly beans into the tea and took a drink. "Talk."

Mint opened a black bottle and dropped withered frog's legs into the mortar. She crushed them as she spoke.

"All I know is when we first met Morgan and Bean, both Licky and I were hooked."

"They were so Southern, from south Georgia, and their accents were smoother than velvet," Licky added. "It was meant to be."

"We loved them at first sight."

"Both of them." Licky dropped her contents beside Mattie, who scooped them up and let them drift into the bubbling cauldron.

"Betty didn't like them," Mint said.

"Of course not." I sipped my tea. "She used to wait up for me with a shotgun strapped across her knees."

Mint laughed. "You're lucky. With us she wore a grenade jacket."

I barked a laugh. "You're kidding."

Licky nudged her sister. "She is, but it wasn't much better. Our mother swore a hex on any boy who dated us."

"Did she do it?"

They exchanged another look.

"Well?" I said.

Licky grimaced. "We don't know."

"We never had any proof," Mint said. She swatted the air. "But that's not what mattered. What mattered was what happened next."

"Which was?"

Licky smiled like it was the best memory on earth. "We eloped."

"The four of us," Mint said. "Went to Witch Vegas and married."

"Why?"

Mint's mouth pursed in anger. "Because our mother wouldn't allow the relationship. She told us that if we insisted on dating those boys, that we'd be thrown out."

"But we were in love," Licky said. "So in love and so young. And they were good boys. They really were. Loved us so fiercely their hearts ached."

"That's what they said," Mint said. "We believed them."

Licky elbowed her. "Of course we believed them. It was the truth."

Mint didn't look convinced. "Anyway, got married and both of us ended up carrying children at the same time."

"That's when it started." Mint dropped something in my mortar. I pestled it without peeking. No telling what it was—lizard brains, maybe.

It sure did crunch. "That's when what started?"

"When their powers blossomed." Mint paused. "See, Morgan and Bean knew they were half genie, but they didn't know if their abilities would come in."

"Sometimes they don't," Licky said. "Not with halfsies."

"But when their genie powers flared, their wishing ability went haywire," Mint explained.

"How so?"

Licky hitched a shoulder. "I'd say something like, I wish my bacon were crisper."

"And instead of crisp bacon, the bacon on her plate would disappear and be replaced with raw bacon," Mint said.

"Ew," was all I managed.

"That's just the beginning," Licky said, sighing. She cupped her chin in her hands. The deep sorrow in her voice made my heart lurch.

"One time Mint wished she'd get her pre-baby body back and she instantly gained fifty pounds."

My eyes flared. "This is a horror story. This isn't a love story."

Mint laughed. "Yeah. Anyway, that's when our chaos powers got worse."

My hair almost stood on end. "Worse?"

Licky nodded. "Our powers were almost controllable before we married Bean and Morgan."

"But once the genie gene kicked in," Mint said, "our abilities flared."

"The mixture of two chaos witches with two bumbling genies was not a good one."

Mint knuckled a tear from her lashes. "So we did the only thing we could."

Licky squeezed Mint's shoulder. "We left. There wasn't a choice."

"How could we raise babies around them? What if something happened to Cordelia and Amelia?"

"It would've been an accident," Licky clarified.

"Of course," I said, completely understanding.

Mint rubbed her forehead. "But we did what we had to for the sake of the girls."

"We haven't seen our husbands in years," Licky said.

Her face crumpled. Mint placed her arms around her sister. Overwhelming sadness flooded my body. The pain these two must've endured. They'd loved their husbands so much. It wasn't like they'd decided to up and leave them because they were bad men.

They couldn't control their abilities—none of the four were able to. They were all perfect for one other. But imagine the chaos that would rock Magnolia Cove if all four of them were in the same room?

A black hole would probably appear and suck the whole town into it.

I shivered.

"Have Bean and Morgan ever wanted to meet their daughters? You know, now that they're grown?"

Mint nodded. "They've been pestering us. But I don't know…"

"See," Licky explained, "it's complicated."

I crossed my arms. "Because you never bothered to tell your daughters the truth and now you're afraid to?"

Mint twisted her fingers. "They might disown us."

"Cordelia would." I wasn't joking. I knew my cousin well enough to guess that she'd be ticked to high heaven about this secret.

Secrets. So many secrets in Magnolia Cove.

Some of them good, some of them bad. Were there any good secrets? Yes, the town itself was actually an awesome secret. But some of the others? I wasn't so sure about them.

"So what am I supposed to do?" I raked my fingers down my face. "You've told me this. I wish I didn't know it. Now I have to keep my mouth shut around them?"

They exchanged a coy glance.

"What?" I fumed.

"We need you," Mint said.

Licky wrapped a hand around my arm. "To watch them."

"If anything changes in our daughters, we want you to tell us."

I swallowed a knot. "So I'm supposed to spy. Watch to make sure their genie gene doesn't turn on. If it does, report back?"

Mint clapped. "You understand completely."

"How wonderful of you to agree." Licky smiled widely.

"I didn't agree."

"But you have to," Mint said.

Licky grimaced. "We can't tell Betty. First thing, she'd be spilling the beans to Cordelia and Amelia. They'd be so angry with us for keeping this from them."

Betty would tell them. She'd tell Cordelia and Amelia for their own safety. I hated the position I'd been placed in. Betray my aunts or betray my cousins.

"Betty doesn't know exactly what happened?" I said.

"No." Licky pulled her red hair over one shoulder. "She knows we left Bean and Morgan, but we never told her about their powers."

"She would've killed us," Mint said. "She never thought it was smart to wed outside of witches. It was one thing for your mother to marry a regular person. She still didn't like it, but she dealt with it. But a genie?"

"There had never been any in Magnolia Cove—not halfsies," Licky explained. "The men kept it a secret. Witches wouldn't have known what to do with them."

"But it doesn't matter," Mint said. "The main thing we want to know is this—if either one of our girls start to develop the ability to grant wishes, will you let us know?"

How had I gotten roped into this again? And why did I think it was a good idea to pal up with my aunts?

Never again.

Amelia and Cordelia had welcomed me into their home like a sister. They'd been good to me, and I would repay them by spying and revealing to my aunts that their daughters had genie powers.

What if the powers never even flared? It was a possibility. If I told my cousins what I knew and their powers didn't work, they'd probably think I was lying.

"Okay," I said, sighing. "I'll watch them."

My aunts started clapping.

"On one condition," I said sharply.

They paused, glanced at me.

"If their fathers want to meet them, you let it happen. My cousins deserve to know their dads. You're not being fair to them."

Licky and Mint exchanged facial expressions in a way that made me realize they were silently talking to one another. After about thirty seconds of eyebrows rising, lips twitching and noses wrinkling, they finally stopped.

"Okay," Mint said, "we will work on allowing the girls to meet their fathers. But one thing you should know—"

"We worry the meet up will flare their powers," Licky finished. "We're not positive it will happen, but it's a definite possibility."

"Sometimes," I said quietly, "you have to take a chance. You have to put everything on the line and dive in."

Mint nodded. "We promise to try to get them together. But you have to do your part. You have to watch our daughters for any sign they have the power and report back."

"Okay," I said. "I will. Now. Where are we on this potion? We need to get this in the mouths of the residents."

Mint looked at everything laid out in front of her. "We're almost done. Pepper, dump the contents of your bowl in here."

I did as she said. "Licky, I need your help."

My aunts joined hands. Mint whispered words of healing while Licky chanted low.

A bubble of magic ignited in their palms. It flew around the room, bouncing from wall to wall.

Mint watched it and smiled. Finally she took the last of the ingredients and dumped them in the boiling cauldron.

Mattie scampered from her spot and jumped into my arms. I held her close as the power flew and bounced. Mint raised her hands and her voice. Licky joined her.

The ball darted into the cauldron. It hissed like a fire fighting to survive. A large bubble rose onto the surface and popped, fizzing slowly back down.

The contents settled. Mint kicked the fire out. She fisted her hands to her hips and smiled. "It's all done."

"Wow. That was fast. But how're we going to serve all this to the residents? It's liquid and I don't see that many bottles?"

Licky smiled. "Easy. We're going to turn it into brownies."

With that, my aunts waved their hands over the cauldron. When they jerked them back, the open mouth of the black cast-iron vessel was filled with brown yummy-looking brownies.

I was impressed.

I stretched the kinks from my back. "Great. Let's go deliver some brownies to the townsfolk."

EIGHTEEN

*W*e handed out the brownies old-school style—by going door-to-door. I'm sure there could've been a faster, better way, but when it came right down to it, I wanted to make sure every person who was sick had a brownie. The best way to do that was to dole them out by hand.

Worked for me, anyway.

For what it was worth, Collinsworth and Mattie walked diligently alongside us. The rabbit kept track of which houses we'd already hit, and Mattie made commentary.

"I sure hope this works," she said.

"Me too. It was the best shot we had considering Farinas stole all the others."

"Correction, she had a warrant to confiscate them," Collinsworth said.

"Same gosh darn thing." There were twenty brownies left. "We can hit between five and ten more houses. Then we need to restock from Mint and Licky."

"Sounds like a plan," Mattie said.

We emptied our basket and headed back home. Mint and Licky

said they would finish the rest. I was grateful. The last couple of days had worn me slap out.

To be honest, I'd been pretty worried about Betty. Amelia had been texting me updates, but I wanted to make sure for myself that she was doing better.

Turned out, I needn't have worried. I opened the front door to find Betty standing at the hearth making beef stew. My stomach rumbled. I couldn't remember the last time I'd eaten.

As soon as I dropped my purse to the floor, Betty wrapped me in a hug. "Good to see you, kid. I was afraid you'd run away."

I pulled back. "Why would I do that? You don't still have a fever, do you?" I pressed the backs of my fingers to her forehead.

"I don't have any cotton-pickin' fever. I was just worried, okay? Can't a grandmother worry about her grandchild without being dragged over coals about it?"

"Sure thing. How're you feeling?"

"Much better."

I smiled. I mean really smiled. My heart swelled. My chest was so tight I think it squeezed tears from my eyes.

Betty fisted her hands to her hips. "Well, you ready for dinner?"

I knuckled the stupid tears away and laughed. "Yep. I'm ready for dinner."

I'd spent most of my Friday working on the spell with Mint and Licky, who I hadn't heard from in the past few hours. Cordelia and Amelia were both at home and came down for dinner. Cordelia looked better. Her cheeks were flushed pink, and there was color on her lips.

Betty heaped a slopping ladle of stew onto my plate. "Do you want to tell us what happened?"

I glanced at Collinsworth, who sat on a stool nimbly munching a carrot.

Yes, in fact I did want to tell Betty. It had been too much to carry around.

"Lori Lou Fick was selling love potions out the back of her store."

Betty dropped her spoon. "What?"

I pointed my cornbread toward Collinsworth. "She spelled a slew of pies with a giving spell that went crazy. That's why you've been wanting to give things away. Problem was, the withdrawals nearly killed you along with half the town. So that's what we'd been working on. With Mint and Licky."

"And the spell worked?" Cordelia said. "With our mothers involved?"

I laughed. "Surprisingly, yes."

My shoulders felt heavy. Like there was a burden I couldn't push off for the life of me.

"How do you know all this about Lori Lou?" Betty said.

"The rabbit told me."

My grandmother chewed quietly. I wasn't supposed to say it. Normally I could keep a secret, I really could, but this wasn't a secret worth keeping.

But at the same time, wouldn't justice work itself out? Wouldn't it all happen the way it was supposed to? Surely it would.

I guess I'd seen too many movies where an innocent person was convicted. I couldn't keep it in any longer.

"Garrick said the murder weapon was covered in Carmen's fingerprints."

I exhaled, waiting for a bomb to fall on me. I'd promised him. Really promised that I wouldn't blurt out that information. But I couldn't keep it in any longer. There was something fishy about it. I knew that. Had to be. My cousin wouldn't kill.

Correction—she hadn't killed.

All gazes settled on me. I stared into my bowl. "I wasn't supposed to say anything." There was no reason for me to be ashamed for trying to help my family.

I hitched a shoulder. "Carmen wouldn't have murdered."

"We all know that," Amelia said. "But the fingerprints? That's terrible. Do you think she touched the scissors because she wanted to see how they cut?"

Cordelia rolled her eyes. "No, she touched them because she likes bright shiny things and couldn't stop herself."

My mouth coiled slightly. Looked like the old Cordelia was back. Good thing. I actually liked her better than the nice one.

Sue me.

"Ha-ha," Amelia said sarcastically. "But why would Carmen have touched them?"

"She didn't." Betty slurped her soup. "They were planted on the murder weapon."

"But," Collinsworth interrupted, "wouldn't the police have discovered that? Surely they would know the difference between a planted fingerprint and one there naturally."

"Not necessarily," Betty said.

I bit down my smile. This was the Betty I knew. The one who was smarter than everyone else.

"What do you mean?" I said.

She tapped the spoon to the side of her bowl. "Someone very crafty, very smart could've actually peeled Carmen's fingerprints from a surface and deposited them on the murder weapon."

"How would they do that?" Amelia said.

"Very carefully."

I leaned forward. "I snuck into Becky Ray's house."

The look of shock on my family's face made heat flush my cheeks. "Listen, I'm not exactly proud of it, but if anyone had an actual motive, it was Becky, not Carmen. Seems Lori Lou's potion making had gotten Becky in trouble before." I nudged the rabbit. "Tell them."

Collinsworth cleared his throat. "Yes, it did."

"What'd you find?" Betty said.

"A shoebox filled with Becky's own recipes for potions. Seems she was trying to perfect some. With the whole giving potion fiasco, Becky Ray would've been exposed once again by Lori Lou. If things got bad, Becky had her own potions and could open a bakery without Lori Lou."

"So you think that was the motive?" Cordelia said.

"Seems pretty solid," I said.

"Unless Becky's the one who placed the giving potion," Amelia said.

The air thickened. All conversation stopped as we looked at her. My cousin shrugged. "What? All I'm saying is, what if it's the other way around and Becky Ray put the potion in the pies instead of Lori?"

"Not possible," Collinsworth said. "It wasn't Becky."

I hitched a shoulder. "That doesn't mean someone didn't plant Carmen's fingerprints on the murder weapon. The entire town was at the Thanksgiving Turkey Hunt. We saw the fight the two women had. It wouldn't have taken a genius to figure out that if you wanted to pin the murder on someone else, Carmen was the next logical person."

"So Becky still could've dosed the pies," Cordelia said.

"It wasn't Becky," Collinsworth muttered. His little paws shook. Was he angry?

"Was Lori Lou seeing someone?" Amelia said. "We could learn a lot if we knew that."

I turned to the rabbit. "Was she?"

"That is no one's business."

"It is our business," I snapped. "My cousin is sitting in jail. That information matters."

"So we go back to Becky Ray's and see if we can figure out if she knew how to steal fingerprints," Amelia said.

"There are certain potions you need," Betty said. "You can't simply steal fingerprints. That's like trying to steal dust."

"So what do you need?" I said.

"Cobwebs," Betty said.

I stopped. Stared at my cousins. "You need cobwebs to steal fingerprints."

She nodded like it was the most logical thing in the world. "Yes, you need bottled cobwebs. Well, usually they're bottled. It makes it easier."

I drummed my fingers on the table. "So all we have to do is find bottled cobwebs and we can at least go to Garrick and give him another suspect, or enough doubt that maybe he'll release Carmen."

Amelia smiled brightly. "Sounds like a great plan."

"Collinsworth?"

He nibbled his carrot. "Yes?"

"Do you know if Becky Ray has bottled cobwebs?"

He shook his head. "No, I don't. She may have kept something like that in her room."

I shook my head. "I didn't find anything like that. What about the bakery?"

He shrugged. "Perhaps. We can check again."

"Oh." I nearly slapped my forehead. "I forgot to tell y'all that after I made the town a batch of cookies, someone stole the healing potion from the bakery."

Their eyes almost fell from their heads.

"What?" Amelia screeched. "It was stolen?"

"I figured it was Becky Ray who did it. But it hasn't been recovered."

Betty tossed her napkin onto the table. "Girls, we've got two things that must be done. The first"—she lifted a finger for emphasis—"is to find the cobwebs. And the second is to find that healing potion. One or both of those will lead us to the killer."

Amelia clapped. "And then we'll know that Becky Ray's the person who tossed the giving potion in all those pies."

"It wasn't Becky Ray!" Collinsworth jumped from his seat. His head bobbed side to side like it might pop off. "It wasn't Becky Ray who put the potion in the pies!"

Cordelia whipped her blonde hair over one shoulder. "Then who was it?"

"It was me," he yelled. "I'm the one who dropped the giving potion in the pies."

NINETEEN

*a*nd the revelations just keep coming.

"Why would you do that?" I said.

I wanted to pick up the rabbit and shake him. What was wrong with Collinsworth? Why would he have dumped a big old dose of stupid giving potion in the town's pies and nearly kill half the folks?

The more I thought about it, the angrier I got. I jumped from my chair. "Why would you do that?"

Cordelia rose. "Let him explain."

I pointed a finger at him. "No. This little guy isn't a rabbit. He's a weasel. He's lied at every turn."

I raked my fingers down my face. I wanted to scream bloody murder. He made me so mad I could spit.

But instead I slowed my breathing and placed my palms on the table. "Why did you lie?"

The rabbit cowered. I shook my head and stared at the ceiling in frustration. He wasn't going to play sweet little bunny on me. No way would I let him get away with that. He was a charlatan. A freaking liar.

Why was I the only person who could see that?

"I put it in because the whole thing was my idea."

"Great," I said. "You said you'd told Lori Lou about selling potions, but the giving spell was your idea? Why?"

"Because I thought…" He pawed his whiskers. "Because I thought if we made everyone happy and giving, they'd give us their money easier and we'd be rich."

"So you wanted to steal from the nice folks of Magnolia Cove?"

"I'm sorry. Really I am." He jumped onto the table. "You have to forgive me. I can't help it. Lori Lou was the only human I ever trusted. She was my best friend. I was only trying to help her. I knew Becky Ray would eventually get mad about something and leave. She'd said as much after the last catastrophe. So I thought…I thought we could get ahead."

"By spelling the town." I rubbed a tension knot from the back of my neck.

He looked at me with big watery eyes. "Yes."

"You're unbelievable. It's just one lie after another with you." I tightened my fists and released them. "Okay. We can only move forward from here. We can't worry about what was. We can only move to what is."

Amelia leaned back. "I wished none of this had ever happened."

Every muscle in my body tensed. I stared at my cousin and held my breath. Would the wish come true? Would all of it disappear? After a few seconds I probed the conversation. It was like touching a sore tooth with my tongue. Or like walking past a cotton field full of dry brown stalks and suddenly realizing I'm thirsty.

Or like realizing the one monogrammed purse with a P on it for Pepper just sold to an elderly woman. Oh, and the monogramming machine is broken.

Seriously, I could go on and on.

But nothing happened. Carmen was still in jail, and I was still sitting across from my relatives. My glance darted to Betty, who too was watching Amelia with interest.

Knowledge hit me like a tidal wave of humidity on an August morning. Betty knew. She knew Cordelia and Amelia were half genie.

I almost busted a gut with laughter.

Of course she knew. The fact that Mint and Licky thought they had pulled one over on Betty was ridiculous. I was pretty sure no one could pull anything over on my grandmother.

It made me proud to be her granddaughter.

"So." I exhaled deeply. "What do we do now?"

A spark twinkled in Betty's eyes. "We search the bakery, but this time we look for a bottle of cobwebs."

Cordelia dragged her spoon through the stew. "And if we don't find them?"

"Then we figure out something else." Betty rose. "Come on girls. Put on your black outfits. Let's go inspect the Sweet Witch."

IT WAS LATE by the time we arrived at the Sweet Witch. I glanced across the street and noticed how sad Marshmallow Magic looked. The doors hadn't been opened in days.

I nudged Betty. "Do you think we should go across the street when we're done? Clean up for Carmen?"

She squeezed my arm. "That's a great idea. We'll do that next."

I smiled sadly. But there wasn't time to be worried or sad. We needed to find some evidence that would lock the guilty party—Becky Ray—away for the rest of her life.

I might make sure Collinsworth joined her there for a while. He lied at every turn. Every chance he had. I was positive that he hadn't killed Lori Lou because he wasn't physically capable of it. Otherwise I would've hauled him down to jail and forced him to confess.

Anyway, we made our way inside and started filtering through the cabinets, opening bottles and vials. Since the first magic cabinet had been pretty much wiped out, there wasn't much to go through. Collinsworth led us to the back, where there was a smaller stash of magical items.

"This ones not used as often."

I quirked my mouth. "If Becky Ray had been the person who stole all the original stuff, where did she put it? We didn't find it in her house."

Cordelia blew on an amber-colored square bottle. "She wouldn't have thrown them all away."

"Why not?"

"Tossing out vials full of magical ingredients is dangerous," Amelia said. "They can explode, cause a magical catastrophe—all sorts of things."

"I didn't know that," I said.

"Every day you learn something new," Betty said. "That's how it is when you're a new witch. Anyway, your cousins are right. You can't throw those things in the trash."

"Then where are they?" A loud crash shook the walls. We gaped at each other in horror. "What was that?"

"If I had to guess," Collinsworth said snottily, "it sounds like the moonshine man is testing a new recipe."

"What?"

The rabbit sighed. "He sometimes tries out new recipes. Things explode."

"I'm going to check it out. He might be hurt."

I dusted my hands on my pants and stepped into alley. I yanked the door to Magical Moonshine. Red light flooded the place, reminding me of flames. My pulse jacked.

I rushed in and found Parker Moody sprawled on the floor. A vat of clear liquid sat beside him.

I shook him, trying to remember everything I'd ever learned in a CPR class. "Parker! Can you hear me? Are you conscious?"

I slid my fingers to his neck. There was a pulse. I shook him harder. "Parker!"

He jerked like a wildcat. "What? What is it? Am I dead?"

I stifled a laugh. "No. You're alive. What happened?"

He slid his fingers through his hair and shivered. "It's embarrassing." Parker straightened. "I was working on a new moonshine recipe. Let me just say it had a real kick to it."

I hooked a hand under his arm. "Let's get you up. Can you stand?"

He brushed me away. "Oh yeah. I'm fine."

When he was standing solidly on the ground, I pointed to his phone. "Do you need me to call someone for you? Your wife, maybe?"

He shook his head. "She's kind of mad at me."

"Oh no. For what?"

Me and my stupid big mouth. These were married people problems and were none of my business.

I wanted to bury my head in a jar of molasses. "Sorry. That was none of my business."

He hitched a shoulder. I noted dark circles under his eyes. "No big deal. I just haven't been a great husband lately is all."

"Oh," I said flatly. "Well, as long as everything is okay here…"

He gave me a kind, if not scruffy-cheeked smile. "I'm fine. Trust me. It's not the first time one of my moonshine experiments has gone wrong. Once I was working on a healing moonshine and ended up almost breaking my neck."

I laughed. "Did you ever get the recipe right?"

"Never did, but it made a great mouthwash."

I laughed. Poor Parker Moody, he looked spent by whatever was happening between him and his wife.

I shot him a sympathetic smile. "We're next door if you need anything."

"Late for y'all to be next door."

My mouth opened and shut like a fish. "Yes, well we're working on some things. Anyway, see you around."

I left the shop satisfied that Parker was okay. If he needed any help, he'd call someone—hopefully his wife.

By the time I made it back to the Sweet Witch, all the shelves' contents sat on the floor.

"Wow. Have y'all missed anything?"

"I don't believe so." Collinsworth hopped forward. "We've searched every nook and cranny."

"What if there are nooks and crannies you aren't aware of?" Amelia fisted her hip.

"I believe I would know if there were any I was unfamiliar with," Collinsworth said.

But how would you know if you were *unfamiliar* with them? Don't worry, I kept my mouth shut

Cordelia dropped a rag on the floor. "Good. Because we've searched every square inch of this place and there's no sign of a bowl of cobwebs or anything like that."

Betty pulled her corncob pipe from her pocket and jammed it between her teeth. "We've scoured the whole place. There's nothing else here to find unless one of y'all wants to keep working?"

No one volunteered.

"Let's get out of here," Betty said.

We locked up and headed out. Mattie and Collinsworth led the way. I grabbed Betty's arm.

"Aren't we going to see if there's anything we can do at Carmen's?"

Betty pulled her pipe from her mouth. "Announcement, girls. We're heading to Marshmallow Magic to make sure your cousin's store doesn't need cleaned up. It's been vacant a few days."

Cordelia and Amelia complied. When we reached the front door, Betty pulled a hidden key from a ceramic spider and inserted it in the lock. When she opened the door, the overwhelming scent of sugar trickled up my nose.

It pretty much made me want to grab a jar of jelly beans and see how many I could fit in my mouth at once.

Luckily I stopped myself.

"It doesn't look like anything needs to be thrown out," Amelia said. "Though I could eat some chocolate."

"You don't need any chocolate," Betty snorted.

Cordelia glanced at Betty. "Are you going to spell the place to keep it in stasis?"

Betty rubbed her chin. "Carmen may already have a spell like that on here. Best to leave it alone."

"Oh." Amelia plucked a red urn from the counter and brought it over. "Look at this. It's so pretty. I've never noticed it before."

Cordelia shook her head. "Don't ever place anything shiny in front of Amelia unless you want her to be distracted for at least an hour."

"Now I know what to get her for Christmas."

Cordelia chuckled. She shot me a grin. "We can go in together."

"Sounds great."

Amelia lifted the top of the urn and gasped.

I edged closer. "What is it?"

She tipped it so we could see. "Look." Her eyes glistened with tears.

I immediately understood why. Inside the urn were clots of sticky cobwebs.

I gritted my teeth. "That doesn't make sense. Why would Carmen have these? The person who framed her would've used the cobwebs, not Carmen."

Betty hung her head. That reaction wasn't good. At all.

My shoulders sank. "Betty? What is it?"

No one spoke. Finally Mattie the Cat jumped on the counter. "No one's talking because cobwebs can place fingerprints but they can also erase fingerprints."

I grimaced. "You mean that Carmen might have these because she was planning on getting rid of the ones on the scissors?"

Betty nodded. "That's how it looks, kid."

We were silent. It was Cordelia who spoke first. "We need to hide them."

"But that would be destroying evidence," Amelia said.

Cordelia threw eye darts at our cousin. "Not if we don't destroy it. We'll only be hiding it." She kicked her toe into the floor. "Do you think our cousin is guilty?"

It was a few seconds before I finally spoke. "No." A wave of confidence buoyed inside me. The next time I said it, the words came out forcefully. "No. Absolutely not. I don't think Carmen is guilty. I think the cobwebs are a bad coincidence."

Amelia nibbled her lip. Finally she spat it out. "No. I don't think Carmen is guilty, either."

"Betty?" Cordelia said.

Our grandmother studied each of us. "If I thought Carmen was guilty, we wouldn't be standing here to begin with."

Cordelia puffed up her chest. "So it's decided. I'll take the urn and hide it somewhere it won't ever be found."

She gently took it from Amelia and cradled it in her arms.

The door opened. We turned to see Farinas Harrell standing there, a sheet of paper in her hands.

"Freeze everyone. I have a warrant for those cobwebs. Hand them over."

TWENTY

*W*e had no choice but to leave the urn with Farinas. That woman seriously had a knack for ruining things. Like, really. I was beginning to think she wasn't so much Carmen's lawyer as she was Carmen's nemesis.

Seriously. Her presence annoyed me.

We made it back to the house. I climbed the stairs to my room and nearly fell face-first onto my bed. I didn't bother peeling off my clothes, though I did kick off my shoes before I plunged into sleep.

I awoke stiff with a fissure of pain shooting up the back of my neck. I groaned.

It was Saturday, which meant it was back to work. It was a weekend full of deals, though most of the stores had been closed on Friday because witches liked to shop at the mall on Black Friday. Of course, given that three-quarters of the town had been sick, it wouldn't have surprised me if most of the town hadn't been able to do any shopping.

Which meant having a sale on familiars was a great idea. Specifically, a sale on puppies was even better.

So that's what was going on. I showered, dressed, and ate breakfast, being sure to drag Collinsworth along.

The rabbit didn't want to go. "Becky Ray will be looking for me. She wants to kill me."

"I don't see why. Garrick isn't investigating her."

"You know why," Collinsworth snapped. "I told you."

"You look pretty alive to me."

The rabbit grudgingly followed me to Familiar Place. The sun shone like a star. I swear the entire town looked new and wonderful, as if a dark curse had been lifted.

We arrived at the shop. I pulled out my golden key and unlocked the door. When we entered, the kittens and puppies, birds and mice all yawned to life.

Collinsworth sniffed. "I see you have my kin."

I barked a laugh when he pointed to the bin of rabbits. "Don't worry, they don't talk as much as you do. Besides, they don't use fake British accents, either."

"I beg your pardon?"

I stifled a giggle. "Come on, Collinsworth, you can't fool me. That accent is fake. F-A-K-E."

He hopped onto a stool and twirled around. "It is not."

"Whatever you say." I hooked my jacket on a peg. "Come on. Don't sit down. Help me feed them."

The rabbit blinked. "You want me to lower myself? Lower my standards and shovel kibble?"

"Yes," I said flatly. "I sure do."

Twenty minutes later we had the animals fed and I was ready for the big sale. I cracked my knuckles, made sure my purse was full of jelly beans and waited.

Turned out, I didn't have to wait long. The bell above the door tinkled and in walked the last person I wanted to see—Farinas Harrell.

"Oh no." I crisscrossed my arms as if warding off a vampire. When you think about it, she wasn't far from it. "You're not allowed in here. You can't issue a warrant for my store. No way."

Her heels clicked as she crossed the linoleum. "I'm not here to do that. I'm here to shop."

Now Farinas Harrell wore designer suits, Manolo Blahnik heels, carried a Louis Vuitton purse and had a three-hundred-dollar haircut. What the heck was she doing in my store? In my shop?

"Listen, Ms. Harrell, I know you're trying to help my cousin, but all you've really managed to do is screw things up."

I mean, I was never going to see this woman again. I didn't care what she thought about me. In my opinion she was horrible.

"Really? And who's the attorney in this room?"

I scoffed. "Well you are."

Her gaze washed from my feet to my crown and then back down to my feet. I suddenly remembered I hadn't polished my boots in ages. And boy, there wasn't anything that ticked me off more than someone giving me the once-over. It was so rude. I wanted to throw something at her—like a jelly bean. Too bad they were in my purse.

"Did you ever stop to think that maybe I took those cookies because I want the police to see my client is innocent?"

"The town needed them," I snapped.

She took an intimidating step forward. "Did you ever stop to think that maybe, just maybe I followed you last night because I knew you'd find something that could help Carmen?"

"Wait. What?"

Her voice rose. "And did you ever stop to think that I won't turn the cobwebs in? That maybe they're completely coincidental?"

"No, I didn't stop to think that at all." I frowned. "Wait. Isn't that withholding evidence?"

"I call it being a good attorney."

"Can't that get you disbarred?"

She waved her hand dramatically. "The police will get what they need."

I cringed. Maybe I should talk to my cousin about hiring a new lawyer. Like maybe I should do it sooner rather than later.

I clapped my hands and put on my most professional smile. "So. What can I do for you? What brings you to Familiar Place?"

"I'd like a familiar."

I choked on a gob of saliva. "I'm sorry, we don't sell..." Worms, bats, snakes, evil otherworldly creatures?

But of course I didn't say any of that. Instead I mustered up. "I'm not sure we have what you're looking for."

Her heels *click click clicked* as she walk walk walked. "I'll be the judge of that."

I closed my eyes. This was what I did. I matched witches with their familiars. I wasn't supposed to be judgmental about it. I was supposed to do my job. After an inhale so deep I'm pretty sure I sent oxygen straight to my toes, I smiled.

"Okay. Let's pair you. Tell me what you're looking for."

Farinas raked her fingers through her hair. "Okay. I'm looking for a companion that will make me a better person."

I had to work so hard to hold in my laugh I almost couldn't speak. "We're not fixing you up on a date."

"That's not what I mean," she snapped. "If you're not going to take this seriously, I will take my business somewhere else."

"No. Wait." I grabbed her hand. A jolt of energy zipped down my spine. I closed my eyes and concentrated. Her magic was strong; so were her instincts and weaknesses.

Farinas had a chip on her shoulder. Probably had to work hard to prove she could beat a man in court.

My lids fluttered open. "Walk around and look at the animals."

Farinas took her time. She stopped at the puppies and pulled out an adorable Labradoodle. She pressed her face into its fur.

"So sweet."

"She's funny," the puppy said. Farinas couldn't understand the dog, but I did.

The puppy licked her face, but there was something missing —*the spark.*

You see, when a witch and her familiar meet, the world ignites. Gravity shifts, bones pop, it is a cosmic event. So when the puppy replied simply about Farinas, I knew it wasn't a match.

"Keep looking," I said.

Next Farinas patted the kittens. She scratched under their chins and smiled at them.

"I want to scratch her," one said.

"Keep going." I pushed Farinas gently along.

She came to the birds. "Oh. I hate them."

"Nice. Well then clearly a bird won't be your familiar. Looks like we can skip them."

She circled the entire store without finding one animal she connected to. I was willing to bet that had more to do with Farinas secretly being part lizard than anything else, but I kept that golden nugget to myself.

Her eyes lit on Collinsworth.

A spark flared in her. She didn't see it, but I could feel it. I grabbed her wrist.

"Collinsworth, come here."

"Why? So you can humiliate me more than you already have?"

I gritted my teeth. "If I humiliated you by suggesting your accent is fake, I'm sorry, but it's the truth. Now come here."

The rabbit hopped over. I picked him up. "Presenting, Collinsworth the Magical Rabbit. Collinsworth, meet Farinas."

Farinas pulled away. "But I'm allergic to bunnies. I could never wear their coats."

"I'm deeply sorry for you." Not at all. "Hold him."

Farinas looked like she'd rather run a marathon in Antarctica than hold the bunny, but there wasn't a choice. I opened her palms and dumped Collinsworth in.

He scrambled, trying to plant his feet so he could jump. Farinas looked like she wanted to drop him.

"Stop it, you two," I yelled. "Look at each other."

"But I don't like rabbits," she protested.

"I hate attorneys," Collinsworth stormed.

I hooked a hand behind Farninas's neck while I grabbed Collinsworth by the ears.

That stopped them both. They slowly made eye contact.

Then I swear it was like a chorus of angels broke into song right there in the middle of Familiar Place.

Collinsworth and Farinas glowed. *Glowed,* y'all. I'm not even kidding. They were each frozen by the other. Golden light bounced off both of them, nearly blinding me.

This was the connection. Usually the light only happened when the witch worked magic, but these two had something seriously powerful connecting them—something I'd never seen before.

Maybe Farinas's Southern accent was fake the way Collinsworth's was.

Nah. It was simply the link between witch and familiar that created this sort of power.

I felt it in my bones. My body hummed with light and wonder. I couldn't help but smile at the two beings who'd annoyed me the most in the past few days.

No, I wasn't going to sugarcoat it. They'd annoyed me. Both of them. In fact, there were times when it had seemed like those two had done just about everything in their power to sabotage all the good I was doing.

At least that's how it felt.

So the fact that these two were now looking at each other with hearts in their eyes was nothing short of earth-shattering and totally ironic.

I dropped my hands from them and smiled. "So what do you think?"

Farinas grinned awkwardly. "I've never felt that."

"That's called matching with your familiar." I clicked my tongue for emphasis and basically because I liked the sound it made.

"I never..." Collinsworth stared at the floor. "I've never felt anything like that. Not even with Lori Lou."

Farinas grimaced. "You knew the murder victim?"

"Yes."

She lurched back as if burned. "We can't. You can't be my familiar. It's a conflict of interest."

The bubble of wonderful burst. The joy in the room deflated.

Collinsworth crumpled. Oh no. This little rabbit whose neck I wanted to strangle oh so many times looked like he'd lost a best friend he'd never had—which is pretty much exactly what had transpired.

"I'm sorry," Farinas said. She backed away, nearly twisting an ankle on her stilettos. She clicked her way across the linoleum and out the door before either of us could say a word.

Collinsworth pressed his paws to his eyes. My heart broke for him. I felt so bad, like I'd been hollowed out myself. I guess that's what watching two beings break apart was like—beings who so desperately wanted to be together but for whatever reason, couldn't.

Yep. I was breaking from Axel all over again. My heart was being squeezed to a mound of clay. It was horrible, and for the first time I experienced real sympathy for the rabbit.

"I'm so sorry," was all I managed.

Then I held his little shaking body as he cried.

TWENTY-ONE

I called Betty and asked her to pick up Collinsworth. She appeared ten minutes later wearing what looked like a motorcycle outfit—leather and waist chains.

"Why're you wearing that?"

"I rode my skillet over."

"It's not that cold."

She sniffed. "Speak for yourself, kid."

I pulled her to the side. "The rabbit's upset. Do you mind taking him home for a little while?"

Her gaze washed over the store. "What happened?"

I glanced over my shoulder. Collinsworth sat on a stool hugging his legs. "I'll explain later."

Her bottom lip stiffened. "You can count on me." She paused. "I saw your cousin today."

"Is she doing okay?" Betty's statement put me on high alert. I hoped Carmen was doing great. I wasn't convinced her attorney was working in her best interest, but that was neither here nor there.

Part of me thought Farinas was as crazy as a left-handed clock. The other part of me thought the same thing.

So I guess all of me thought she was loony.

Betty crossed to Collinsworth. "Ever ridden a cast-iron skillet?"

"I can't say that I have." Collinsworth blew his nose.

"Come on. You'll love it." Betty hooked an arm under the rabbit and pressed him to her waist.

I waved goodbye. "See y'all back at the house."

They left and it didn't take long for the next customer to enter.

"Hi...Pepper, isn't it?"

Dicky Downy made his way across the floor, inspecting the animals as he walked.

"Yes. Dicky, right?" Like I didn't know his name. I blew a strand of bangs from my face in agitation. But if Dicky was going to pretend to remember my name, then I would do the same thing to him.

"That's right." He punched his fists into his pockets.

"So what brings you here?" Such a stupid question. I almost slapped my forehead.

"A Christmas present for my niece."

I crossed my arms. Something occurred to me. "You bought a pecan pie with a chocolate bat in it from Lori Lou, didn't you?"

He eyed a black kitten in the cage. "I did. It was for my parent's holiday dinner."

"Did they eat any of it?"

He scratched the scruff on his jaw. "The whole thing."

My jaw nearly collided with the floor. "Did anyone get sick? You know the entire town's been full of folks trying to give things away."

He slowly nodded. "They did. I think they managed to get some of the cookies you were handing out the other day."

"I don't remember seeing you there."

"How much for this cat?"

Good evading, Dicky.

"It's better if you bring your niece in," I said gently. "I match witches with their familiars when the witch is present. I'm not saying you can't buy it, all I'm saying is it's better if I can see the two interact. It makes a better familiar."

So funny. A couple of months ago I would've thought this whole conversation was hogwash, but now I knew every bit of it was true. Every single bit.

"Then maybe I'll bring her in."

I drummed my fingers on the counter. "It was nice of you to sit with Amelia when our grandmother was sick."

"Oh?" He hitched a brow. "She told you that?"

"She mentioned it."

"Shh." He brought his finger to his lips. "Don't tell anyone. It might give the town an aneurysm."

I stifled a chuckle. "Why?"

"Well, you know… Oh, you don't know because you weren't here."

Please, tell me everything. I didn't say it, but I almost did. So close. So very close.

"What don't I know?" I said innocently.

"I used to have a reputation around here."

"No one's perfect." I grinned, trying to be as encouraging as possible.

Dicky ruffled the back of his hair. "In high school I used to sell things I shouldn't have. My parents eventually got wind of it. Because of that, they curbed my activities. I almost got sent to military school."

Wow. My cousins hadn't told me that part. They probably didn't know about it.

"What sort of things did you sell?"

Dicky cleared his throat. "Let's just say if you wanted a guy to fall hard for you, I could make that happen."

So he *had* been selling love potions. "Interesting."

"It almost got me in jail." He hitched a shoulder. "So it wasn't that interesting at all. It was mostly stupid."

"At least you learned your lesson before something bad happened."

He hitched another shoulder.

Tension rose in the room. It was thick, heavy. There was something Dicky wasn't saying. Something that made me want to ask my next question.

"Did something bad happen?"

He raked his fingers through his hair. Whatever it was, Dicky wasn't going to say it.

"Listen, I'm having a party at my new house tonight."

Wait. What?

I must've looked confused because Dicky laughed. "Don't worry. I won't be doing any of my old tricks. No one's handing out potions."

"Great," I said. "Is it just a small gathering?"

"I've invited a lot of the town. It should be fun."

The feeling that Dicky Downy was hiding something gnawed my insides. I wanted to know what it was.

The best place to find that out was in his house—snooping.

I didn't know if Dicky had information that would help Carmen, but why hadn't he been infected with the giving spell like everyone else? He'd bought a pecan pie with a chocolate bat in it. Yes, he said his parents had eaten one of the cookies I'd given out, but I'd recognized everyone at the bakery Friday morning.

Every single face and no one there had the last name Downy.

There was no doubt about it—Dicky Downy was keeping secrets. Secrets that I needed to unearth if I was going to get Carmen out of jail.

Let's face it, Farinas Harrell might be a shark in the courtroom, but nothing she'd done so far had pinned the murder on someone else.

It was time to find the real murderer.

I plastered on a big smile. "Sure, Dicky, I'd love to attend your party. See you tonight."

I CLOSED the store at three after having sold one puppy, one kitten and one rat.

Yes, I sold rats as familiars. Not many witches bought them, but the few that did really loved the little critters.

To each his own, I always say. Or whatever floats your boat.

When I arrived home, I found Cordelia on the couch. The house was quiet.

I pegged my purse. "Where is everybody?"

She glanced up from her crossword puzzle. "They went on a picnic. Collinsworth was crushed. What happened to him?"

I barked a laugh. "Can you believe he paired with Farinas Harrell?"

Cordelia's jaw dropped. "Satanette herself?"

I laughed tears. I knuckled them away and had to catch my breath. "Yes. Her. They matched but she wouldn't take him. So he's devastated. He just lost Lori Lou plus thinks Becky Ray wants him dead for telling me about the potion selling, so he's pretty vulnerable."

"Sounds like it." She tossed the crossword on the table and stretched her arms over her head. "We haven't had a chance to talk."

I slumped onto a chair. "About what?"

She gave me a pointed look.

"Oh." Heat flushed my neck. "You mean Axel."

"Yes, I mean Axel." Cordelia pulled her legs to her and hooked an arm around them. "Plenty of people have brought him up, but none of them have done it the right way." She shook her head. "I'm sorry about my mom and aunt. I wished they'd never said anything at Thanksgiving."

Wow. Lots of wishing going on with my cousins lately. I paused again, waiting to see if something would change. Would I forget that Mint and Licky had mentioned Axel at Thanksgiving?

Nope. Didn't happen.

"They didn't mean it in a bad way," I said.

Cordelia's lip twitched. "Listen, I know it's painful to talk about, but I know the way Axel used to look at you. He loved you, Pepper."

Tears sprang to my eyes. I stared up at the ceiling, wishing them away. Dang it. I wished I possessed wishing powers.

I exhaled a staggered breath. "Yep. He did. He said he loved me."

"I think…" She paused. "I know I'm not the most warm and fuzzy person. I know I act like I don't care about things like feelings."

"Only when it comes to Amelia."

We laughed. My cousin tucked a strand of long blonde hair behind an ear. "I know I'm hard on her. But we're like sisters—we get on each other's nerves. But anyway, all I wanted to say is if you need to talk about Axel, I'm here."

"Thanks, but there's nothing to talk about." I stared at the ceiling again. "He hasn't even called."

"Not for one second do I believe you've heard the last of him."

"I don't know. He just left."

She leaned forward. "You and Axel belong together. You just do. He's coming back. I can feel it. When he got loose and almost killed you, for lack of a better way to say it, it freaked him out. It was too much. That's his worst nightmare, right? Hurting you? He couldn't live with himself if he did something like that."

I hitched a shoulder. "It's what he said. I know there's a way to solve it."

"But he has to figure that out for himself. I've known Axel a long time. I mean, the ladies call him Mr. Sexy, for goodness' sake. He's a man's man. He's all guy, and what guys like to do is solve problems for themselves. It's not enough you telling him it's going to be okay. He has to solve the problem."

I scoffed. "How can he solve this? He becomes a werewolf once a month."

"He will." She studied me. "He can. He'll be back. Don't give up on him. Unless you've already decided you don't want him."

My stomach fell to the floor. "I've—I don't know. I just figured I'd mend my broken heart and never lay eyes on him again. I haven't thought about what would happen if he shows up."

"It's something to think about." She inhaled. "So. What else is going on?"

"Dicky Downy is having a party tonight."

Her eyebrows ratcheted to the sky. "You're kidding?"

"No. I'm sure Amelia knows, doesn't she?"

Cordelia's lips pinched. "Probably. But she hasn't said anything."

I leaned forward. For some reason I felt very conspiratorial. "He came over when you and Betty were sick."

Her mouth puckered. "No, I didn't know that."

"He did."

"Yeah, I'm not a real fan of Dicky. He's okay, but not my favorite person." She paused. "Not that it's any of my business, but I can't believe Amelia let him in." She shook her head in annoyance. "She's always had a thing for him though, ever since..."

Her gaze darted to the side.

"Ever since what?"

Cordelia pulled her hair over one shoulder and started braiding. "I guess it's not a huge secret, it just isn't something we talk about."

"What? Now I have to know."

She sighed. "You know Dicky used to have those parties."

"Yeah. Y'all told me about them."

Cordelia worked on her braid for a moment. Never in my life had I seen my cousin so interested in a plait of hair.

"Are you avoiding telling me?" I nudged.

She smiled. "I was hoping you'd forget we were talking about him."

"No luck there."

"Anyway, Dicky would sell love potions and other stuff at these parties. Well, one time he didn't sell a love potion, he gave it to a girl he really liked."

My stomach twisted. "You're not saying it was Amelia?"

Cordelia nodded. "Yep. Dicky dosed her with a love potion. To be honest I'm not sure if it ever totally wore off."

TWENTY-TWO

*D*icky Downy's party was in full swing. And by swing, I mean swing dancing.

I glanced down at my jeans and boots. "I forgot my poodle skirt."

Cordelia murmured in my ear. "Yeah, someone should've told us to dress up."

Amelia twirled around in her froufrou outfit. "I told y'all there would be swing music."

"No you didn't," I said.

She shrugged. "I thought I had. Oh well."

The house was stuffed full of people. It was stuffy, sweaty and smelled like someone had broken a bottle of wine on the floor.

"Can you hold me?"

I glanced down at Collinsworth. Yes, I know the rabbit wasn't officially invited to the party, and I was sure no one else had brought their pets, but the little guy was still upset about what had happened with Farinas. I guess Lori Lou's death along with the attorney's rejection had been too much for his little heart to take.

I scooped him up. "You're sweaty," he complained.

"Okay. I'm putting you down."

"No!" He scrambled into my arms. "No, that's all right. I'll stay exactly where I am."

"Great."

Dicky Downy wove his way through the crowd. His eyes twinkled when he settled them on Amelia.

"Hey, ladies," he cooed.

"Hey, yourself." Amelia beamed. I'm surprised she wasn't glowing her smile was so bright.

He extended his hand. "You care to join me for a dance?"

Her palm slid over his. "I'd love to."

"Well." Cordelia grabbed a cup of punch off a table. "I guess there they go."

"Is Garrick coming?"

She shook her head. "It's hard for him to attend things like this. You know, everyone acts weird around him. He can't relax."

"Yeah, I can see that."

Cordelia handed me a cup of punch. "It's okay. This way I can keep an eye on Amelia."

"Have you asked her about Dicky?"

"Yeah." She leaned back on her slender hips. "So last time Betty had to get involved and heal her. Of course Dicky had bought the potion from who knows where and God only knew what the heck was in that nasty stuff."

"What do you mean?"

"That's another reason why they're illegal. A love potion could fry your brain. The ingredients aren't regulated. It's like any illegal drug. You never know what it's actually made of. Anyway, Betty helped Amelia. When she got well, I asked how she felt about Dicky."

I sipped on the strawberry-flavored drink. Yum. "What'd she say?"

"Get this—Amelia said he was an okay guy. The jerk had just potioned her and she thought he was okay."

Realization hit me like a swarm of gnats. "So that's why you don't know if she ever fully healed."

"Right. If that happened to you, wouldn't you say he's the biggest jerk ever?"

"Yep. You shouldn't have to potion someone into loving you."

Cordelia studied me. "No, you shouldn't." Her gaze swept over our cousin, who was gleefully dancing with Dicky. "I just wish she realized that."

I hitched a shoulder. "Maybe she does. Maybe we're not giving her enough credit."

"Maybe." Doubt dripped from her voice. It was so thick I was surprised I didn't see it land on the floor. Of course, I don't know what it would've looked like. Little letters? Or more like a dry cracker?

Okay, enough of the indulging thoughts.

Collinsworth pawed my neck so hard it felt like claws were digging in.

"What?" I pulled him off. "What's wrong?"

"Becky Ray." He pointed across the room. "She's here. She wants to kill me."

"She doesn't want to kill you. Will you settle down?"

Becky Ray scanned the crowd. Her laser-beam gaze landed on us. When it did, her face twisted into a hideous grimace. Red flushed her flesh. She fisted her hands to her sides and stalked across the dance floor toward us.

The point I'd argued with the rabbit—that Becky Ray didn't want to harm him—got thrown out the window.

Becky Ray looked like she wanted to kill.

Correction, she looked like she wanted to throttle, maim and toss him over a bridge—times one hundred thousand.

"We have to go," Collinsworth said.

For once I believed him. I nudged Cordelia. "I think Becky Ray's going to kill the rabbit. We're getting out of here."

Cordelia winked. "I got your back, sweet tea witch. I'll stall her."

As I raced from the party, I heard Cordelia. "Hey, Becky Ray. You look great tonight. Do something different with your hair?"

I sprinted from the house. Collinsworth clutched my shirt. "Hurry. She's going to kill me!"

"We're out the door."

"Becky Ray won't stop until she finds me." For some reason the rabbit was panting. Why was he panting? I was the one doing all the work.

"I'll hurry."

I took a moment to glance behind me. Sure enough, freakazoid Becky Ray was speed walking down the street like the Terminator. I fully expected her to drop her human arms and reveal bionic limbs.

"Rabbit, I need to talk to you!"

It sounded more like a warning than a cuddly invitation to tea. I hugged him close. "I won't let her get you."

I raced down the street and realized I'd really let my running drop off. I needed to get back into it. It wasn't like I didn't have time because I was busy going on any hot dates.

A stitch ticked up my side. We were on Bubbling Cauldron. A line of shops greeted us.

"Go to the bakery," Collinsworth whispered.

"She'll be on us like white on rice." Was he kidding? Wasn't it the first place she would look?

"You can call the police from there. We'll lock the door. Hurry!"

I raced to the alley and opened the door. It was unlocked. I dropped Collinsworth on the floor and propped a chair against it, hoping that would stop Becky Ray.

It didn't.

The front door screeched open. I shot Collinsworth a terrified look. "Quick, the closet!"

How original of me. We started to dash in that direction when Becky's voice stopped us.

"Hold it right there."

I put my hands up like she was holding a gun to my back. I wasn't even looking at her, y'all, but I figured she probably had a gun or something. Why else would she have said hold it?

I shot Collinsworth a terrified look. The poor rabbit had his back to me. He trembled with fear. This Becky Ray had no business harming an innocent rabbit. Okay, he wasn't that innocent, but he was still only a small bunny. She needed to pick on someone her own size.

I gritted my teeth and turned around. Yes, I still had my hands up.

Becky Ray stood with legs splayed wide and a knife in her hand. "Rabbit, you are dead."

"Stop it," I said.

Becky Ray, her curly hair looking like fried hay, shot me a startled look. "I can do whatever I want. That rabbit betrayed me."

"No, you can't." I stamped my foot. "It's illegal to harm animals. But from the way you're holding that knife, I wouldn't be surprised if you were the person who killed Lori Lou."

Yes, I said it. Someone needed to.

Becky Ray's face twisted in rage. "Why you—"

She didn't finish her sentence. She shot forward. The knife descended in an arc. It would plunge into my chest. I couldn't think. I couldn't breathe. Y'all, I couldn't form one coherent thought except, *knife!*

That didn't help anything.

Suddenly something hit Becky Ray on the top of the head. She slumped to the ground. The knife clattered across the floor, coming to rest under the counter.

I exhaled a shaky breath. I glanced up to see Parker Moody standing where Becky had been. He held a cast-iron skillet. A real one, not one for riding.

I reached for him with trembling hands. "Oh my gosh. Thank you. You saved us. She was going to kill us both. I think she murdered her sister."

Parker slid a hand over his jaw. "Let me tie her up and I'll call the police."

A few minutes later Collinsworth and I stood in Magical Moonshine. Parker had hung up with the police, who would be arriving in a few minutes.

"Thank you so much," I said. "You saved us."

"Yes, thank you," Collinsworth said.

"No problem." Parker motioned to a jar. "I'd offer you some moonshine, but I figure you'd probably prefer something stronger, like coffee."

I laughed. "Yeah." Parker was nice. He had a friendly face and a kind smile. I hoped he worked out his differences with his wife. He deserved it. He'd saved me from a murderer.

My cell phone rang. For some reason, even amid all the craziness, I still had my purse slung over my shoulder and my phone in it.

"Excuse me."

I recognized the number immediately. "Hello?"

"Pepper, do you have a minute?"

I didn't want to encourage Rufus, but he had been helpful. "What is it?"

"Listen, I found out a little more about Lori Lou."

I shot Parker a smile. He was busy wiping down a counter. "I think that business is all cleared up."

"No, listen. I discovered that Lori Lou did leave her last town because of the potion business gone wrong, but she came to Magnolia Cove because she was seeing someone."

I pressed the phone closer to my ear. "So what? Why is that important?"

He sighed. "According to people, she kept her relationship quiet because the man was involved with someone else. It may have been a motive for murder."

I numbed. My fingers, my toes, my core—all of me went numb. "Okay. Thank you."

"Be careful, Pepper."

I thumbed off the phone. The slip of paper with the phone number on it. I was wearing the same jeans as yesterday. No, I hadn't washed them because jeans didn't get dirty quickly, everyone knew that. You could wear a pair several times before washing. That was hand-to-heart gospel truth—ask anyone, even a Baptist. They might not drink in public or dance, but they let their jeans dirty before washing.

The slip of paper was still in my pocket. My fingers trembled. My thumb slipped a couple of times as I dialed.

"Everything okay?" Parker said.

"Oh yeah." I stared at my phone and pressed Send.

Another cell in the room rang. And rang. And rang.

"Is that yours?" I said to Parker. "It might be your wife."

He pulled it from his pocket and glanced down. "Not her." His face darkened. "I know it's you, Pepper. Put the phone down."

"Pepper," Collinsworth squealed.

When I looked up, Parker Moody had a gun leveled at me. Why didn't anyone use magic to hurt anyone else in this town? It never ceased to amaze me that in a cove full of witches, the main instruments of death were knives and guns.

Time to get original, people.

"You stole the potion," I said.

He smirked. "It was all I ever wanted. Lori Lou told me about it. You think I wanted to date her?"

"You're evil," the rabbit said. "She was a wonderful person."

Parker waved the gun at Collinsworth. "Stand beside Pepper."

The rabbit did as he was told.

The puzzle clicked together. "That night when something exploded, you were working with the potion."

He smiled again. "It can be volatile. Took me a while to figure out which bottle it was in and then how to perfect it. Like I told you, I'd been working on a healing moonshine. Bottling that will make me a millionaire."

"At the expense of someone else's life."

He scowled. "We argued the day of the turkey hunt. She wouldn't give it to me. Yes, I killed her. I lifted Carmen's fingerprints from her store. It was easy to frame her. I also placed the cobwebs back in her shop to keep suspicion off me."

"And the other argument you had with Lori Lou? The one about the trash bags?" The front door was far away and Parker weighed a good one hundred eighty pounds. There was no way I could dash past him with the rabbit.

"All the other arguments were for show. No one could find out about us. My wife suspected; that was enough."

"You won't get away with this," I said. "The police are on their way."

He crossed and blocked the front of the door. "All I have to do is kill you and say you left before the police arrived. Then I'll dispose of your bodies later. The rabbit will be easy." He smiled like the devil. "I love stew."

"You evil man." Collinsworth launched himself at Parker. The moonshine maker opened his hand and swatted the rabbit away.

"Good try, Bugs." Parker smiled with amusement. "But you're no match for me."

The rabbit wasn't, but I should've been. After all, I was a head witch. I could make whatever magic happen that I wanted. All I needed was to believe it.

I wanted to shove Parker into his own moonshine. The guy deserved it.

I thought him against the wall. Parker didn't just stumble backward, he flew across the room and smashed into a triangle of glass jars.

Glass shattered and exploded. Purple- and lime-colored moonshine spewed over the floor, making a giant puddle around Parker.

This was my chance. I grabbed Collinsworth and raced to the door. I was a foot from it, my fingers stretched to grab hold when Parker's voice rang out.

"Not so fast."

I was frozen. I couldn't move. Whatever magic Parker had, it was stronger than mine.

A wet hand wrapped around my neck. "You're not going anywhere, Pepper. You're mine."

TWENTY-THREE

*P*arker Moody had me. I was going to die, Collinsworth would become stew and Carmen would go to jail for a crime she didn't commit. Unless Farinas got her off the hook.

I doubted it.

Parker dragged me across the room. I kicked and yelled. I tried to focus on pushing him away, but my mind was shattered. There were so many thoughts. I'd never see my family again. I'd never talk to Axel.

Axel.

No one would know what happened to me. That single thought filled me with anger. Anger I didn't know I owned.

I was angry that Axel just left, angry that Parker would win, angry that my hair would look awful when I died.

Yes, girl, I wanted to look good in death. I didn't want to look bad.

Suddenly Parker's hands were off. I whirled around to face him. I was a volcano of regret, frustration and pure unadulterated rage.

"You don't get to win, Parker."

I thrust out my arms. Parker flew to the wall. He straightened, shook himself off and launched toward me.

His hands wrapped around my throat. I fell backward. I kneed him in the groin. He moaned and rolled off.

Rope. I needed rope.

He swept his arm under my feet. I hit the floor. Pain radiated from my tailbone to my jaw. I kicked but he grabbed.

I tried to push away the pain, but it all came crashing down. I got one knee under his chin and knocked his head to the side.

I rose stiffly to my feet.

The look of pure hatred in his eyes made my blood freeze. "You're mine now."

"No, she's not."

My heart stopped. I couldn't move. Every cell in my body recognized that voice. It was the one thing I'd yearned to hear over the past few weeks. The one sound that always soothed me, righted me, made everything perfect when I heard it.

I held my breath because this wasn't real. It couldn't have been real. I didn't want the moment to be ruined, but I had to look. I had to know.

My gaze slowly lifted to the doorway.

Axel Reign stood inside Magical Moonshine. The waffle-patterned shirt he wore fit him like a second skin. His jeans were slung low. His hair was a little longer, his face a little gaunt, but his blue eyes burned with fire.

Our gazes locked. My stomach fell into the earth. It was probably on its way to China, never to be seen again.

Also, I couldn't breathe. I didn't know where that had gone, either. It was somewhere floating around space probably. I might suffocate. Axel might have to give me mouth-to-mouth.

I could deal with that.

His lips twitched. "Hey." It was husky, low. My knees wobbled.

"Hey," I squeaked like a mouse.

Way to sound sexy, Pepper.

Parker stretched. Oh, was he still here? "I can take you both."

A silly thought entered my head. I cocked my chin to Axel. "Do you really think he can take us both?"

"No. He can barely handle you."

I scoffed. "I was losing."

"Don't sell yourself short. You were coming back."

I laughed. "You think?"

When his lips tipped into a luscious smile, I almost died. "You had it, Pepper. I was only going to help wrap him up for you."

Parker moved to do something. Without turning from me, Axel raised a hand, palm open. Parker froze.

I giggled. "You are so powerful."

His blue eyes twinkled. "What can I say? You inspire me."

Parker seethed. "I will break this hold."

Axel shook his head slightly. "I doubt it." His gaze washed over me from head to foot. It didn't bother me when Axel looked at me like that. It made me feel good, like he was seeing inside me.

"I'm sorry I left." He took a step forward.

"It hurt. It still hurts."

"I will get out," Parker said.

Axel moved his other hand in a horizontal line like he was closing an imaginary zipper. "That should keep him quiet." A dark shadow crossed his face. "I know I hurt you. I'm sorry. I'm so, so sorry."

I cocked my head but said nothing.

He exhaled. "Look, I'm not good at this. You know I'm not. Relationships terrify me. You terrify me."

"Ouch."

His lips coiled. "In a good way. When I was gone, I ached for you. Every part of me missed you. I realized what a god-awful mistake I had made. *I need you.*"

My knees trembled.

Axel took another step forward. "Without you, I was only a shadow of myself. I couldn't eat. I couldn't think. I couldn't get enough air. You are air to me, Pepper. You are my life force."

Whoa.

He took another step. Axel wasn't even breaking a sweat keeping his power focused on Parker.

He slid a hand over my cheek. Fire lit from my belly all the way to my crown. No one touched me like this. There was some weird thing with Rufus, but Axel's touch was like he said—it was life.

There was no comparison.

"Like I said," Axel continued, "I'm not great at relationships, but without you, I am nothing. You are my everything." He stopped, looked away. A shadow of a smile graced his face. "I know I don't deserve it. I left. I was scared. If you tell me right now that we're over, I'll understand."

The world was crashing down. Here Axel stood telling me everything I'd wanted to hear, everything I had hoped in my heart. The earth shifted and I was falling. There was only one person who could catch me.

He was standing right in front of me.

"I...I..." Words sounded so stupid, so small in comparison to the swelling of my heart. There wasn't a phrase or a saying that could envelop what I felt and what I wanted.

"I missed you so much." The words caught in my throat. They came out with a half sob. My gaze darted away. The emotion was too much. It was more than I could handle.

No. It wasn't. I could do this. I'd endured so much in his absence. Axel's rightful place was beside me. He needed to know that. The words would come. I only had to trust.

"You abandoned me." Okay, not the start I expected.

Axel grabbed my hands. "I was wrong. I ran away from you and myself when I should've been running toward you and only you."

The crushing feeling returned. I nodded slightly. My noggin felt like a stupid bobblehead. "You left."

Still I kept bringing up the past when he wanted the future. It couldn't be helped. I'd waited so long to talk to him. These were the words that needed to spill from my gut.

"I will never, ever leave you again. I was hopeless without you. I am hopeless. My heart was broken. I did it to myself when I never should have."

My own heart hurt from his words. His pain was mine, and I hated it.

"Do you know how many times I saw something and said, 'Wow, Pepper would love that'?" He glanced at the floor. "This is so stupid, but I carried around a bag of jelly beans in my pocket the whole time I was gone."

"You should've asked for a lock of hair."

He barked a laugh. His beautiful blue eyes darted to the ceiling. "I should have. I have been so foolish, Pepper. So stupid and foolish. Will you forgive me?"

"Can I see the jelly beans?"

He slid a hand into his pocket. When he pulled it out, he revealed a crumpled ziplock bag of my favorite flavors.

"That lemon looks really good right now."

He dropped them in my palm and closed his hand over mine. "They're all yours."

His gaze hooked mine like a spear to my spine. My breath staggered.

"Pepper Dunn, I love you. Will you forgive me?"

So many thoughts, so many, but the only one that mattered was the one that fell from my lips in that moment.

"There's nothing to forgive."

He slipped his hands around my waist and pulled me into a soft, breathless kiss that could've lasted forever. Seriously, the world could've burned down around us, but all that would've mattered was that Axel was back and I loved him.

We stopped kissing when the front door opened. I slid my hands from Axel's neck and let him hold me protectively as we whirled to face who had entered the store.

"Hey, Axel, Pepper," Garrick Young said. "Got a call about an attempted murder?"

Axel pointed to Parker Moody. "He's right there. Pepper can tell you everything."

TWENTY-FOUR

I explained everything to Garrick Young while Axel held my hand and stroked the inside of my elbow.

Frankly, it made it impossible to concentrate.

Garrick arrested Parker Moody for the murder of Lori Lou and also arrested Becky Ray for Collinsworth's attempted murder.

She had wanted to kill the rabbit after all. Turned out the mob was pretty ticked that their supply of potions was going to be gone, so Becky had tried to make up her own recipes but couldn't get it quite right. To get rid of all the evidence, she decided to get rid of Collinsworth, too.

I probably would've been next.

And the rabbit got his happily ever after as well. Carmen was released, and Farinas came to her senses and realized she couldn't live without Collinsworth.

Thank goodness because I didn't have room for one more pet in my house. A dragon and a talking cat were quite enough.

"I'll miss you."

It was the next day and Collinsworth stood on the porch. He wore Lori Lou's handkerchief around his neck and a brand-new set of clothes that Betty had whipped up for him.

Granted, it was a monogrammed sailor-boy outfit, but beggars couldn't be choosers.

I think my grandmother thought the rabbit was a real boy underneath all that fur.

Maybe his nose grew, too, when he told a lie.

I cuddled him to my chest. "I'll miss you."

"Thank you."

He turned to leave. "Wait. Did you drop your British accent?"

I swear he blushed. "Yes."

"Will wonders never cease." I kissed the top of his head and settled him on the porch.

He took my hand. "I will always remember you, Pepper Dunn."

"And I'll always remember you."

Farinas was waiting for him beside her car. He hopped away, to his new life. I smiled as the attorney whisked him into her arms and tucked him into his brand-new car seat.

Probably made for a toddler, but whatever. The rabbit was happy. That was all that mattered.

Amelia stepped onto the porch. She stretched her long arms over her head. "How're you doing?"

"Good. Great. How're you? How's Dicky?"

She hitched a shoulder. "You know, for as crazy about him as I was in high school, it seems that those feelings are gone." She arched her back and rolled her shoulders. "I never thought it was possible, but it's happened."

"I'm sure Cordelia's happy."

She smirked. "Ecstatic."

I laughed. A cool breeze blew across the porch. I hugged my arms and tugged my cardigan tighter. "I guess things are finally getting back to normal."

Amelia smiled. "I think so. Listen, I'm going for a run. I'll see you later."

She sprinted down the steps and was off. I inhaled the crisp fall air and smiled. Things had indeed gotten back to normal.

An SUV I didn't recognize rumbled to the curb. It was an older model and was decked out for what looked like a guided tour through the Savannah. There was a ladder on the back, a rack on top, big tires.

I'd never seen it before. I wondered if Garrick had gotten a new vehicle.

The door opened, and Axel crossed around the nose of the vehicle. "What is that?" I said.

He smiled at me. The world bloomed inside my chest. "You like it? I got rid of the truck and the mustang for it. It's older. Needs some work. I'm slowly restoring it."

"It's cool. Rugged. Like you."

He stopped on the sidewalk and gazed up at me. Thick, dark lashes framed his cool blue eyes. We stared at each other.

"I didn't see that vehicle last night."

"Last night you needed me to walk you home."

I nodded. He had and I did. I needed as much time with Axel as I could get. So I could imprint every part of him on me.

Not in a weird way, but more of in a sentimental one. Once I'd admitted to myself how I felt about him, I didn't want him absent in my life.

He jiggled his keys. "So. You got dinner plans tonight?"

I took one step down.

He approached a few paces.

"No, I'm free."

We stood so close I could feel the heat radiating from him into me. I was like a sponge, absorbing his energy and life force.

Axel threaded his fingers through mine. He lifted his face and gently kissed me, tugging at my lips.

We parted. He smiled. The world ignited when he said, "Well then, it's a date."

It certainly was.

ALSO BY AMY BOYLES

SWEET TEA WITCH MYSTERIES

SOUTHERN MAGIC

SOUTHERN SPELLS

SOUTHERN MYTHS

SOUTHERN SORCERY

SOUTHERN CURSES

SOUTHERN KARMA

SOUTHERN MAGIC THANKSGIVING

SOUTHERN MAGIC CHRISTMAS

SOUTHERN POTIONS

SOUTHERN GHOST WRANGLER MYSTERIES

SOUL FOOD SPIRITS

HONEYSUCKLE HAUNTING

BLESS YOUR WITCH SERIES

SCARED WITCHLESS

KISS MY WITCH

QUEEN WITCH

QUIT YOUR WITCHIN'

FOR WITCH'S SAKE

DON'T GIVE A WITCH

WITCH MY GRITS

FRIED GREEN WITCH

SOUTHERN WITCHING

Y'ALL WITCHES

HOLD YOUR WITCHES

SOUTHERN SINGLE MOM PARANORMAL MYSTERIES

The Witch's Handbook to Hunting Vampires

The Witch's Handbook to Catching Werewolves

The Witch's Handbook to Trapping Demons

ABOUT THE AUTHOR

Amy Boyles grew up reading Judy Blume and Christopher Pike. Somehow, the combination of coming of age books and teenage murder mysteries made her want to be a writer. After graduating college at DePauw University, she spent some time living in Chicago, Louisville, and New York before settling back in the South. Now, she spends her time chasing two preschoolers while trying to stir up trouble in Silver Springs, Alabama, the fictional town where Dylan Apel and her sisters are trying to master witchcraft, tame their crazy relatives, and juggle their love lives. She loves to hear from readers! You can email her at amy@amyboylesauthor.com.

Made in United States
Orlando, FL
01 July 2023

34654069R00107